MOVING ON

MOVING ON

BARBARA LUDMAN

modjaji books

Published in 2024 by Modjaji Books
Cape Town, South Africa
© Barbara Ludman

www.modjajibooks.co.za

This is a work of fiction. All the characters,
organisations and events portrayed in this novel are
either products of the author's imagination or are used
fictitiously.

ISBN 978-1-991240-29-3

Editor: Pat Tucker
Cover design: Jesse Breytenbach
Text design and layout: Liz Gowans

For Arlyn and Ann, and the TLC

Contents

1

Bridging the gap

Esther

It was the comment on peas that did it.

"He said: 'You haven't finished your peas.' There were seven peas left on the plate."

"You counted them?"

"Maybe six peas. How many peas can you eat? I'd had enough. But he'd paid for my meal and expected me to finish it. And be grateful. Grateful! I could buy and sell him six times over."

Esther had been on her own for a year when she gave in to her friends' matchmaking attempts. They didn't have to work very hard to convince her. She hadn't been entirely abandoned to her four-bedroom home plus cottage/ guestroom. One daughter was overseas but another was only half an hour away, and her son was even closer, but her children, let's face it, had their own lives.

There were bridge lessons – all women – and she lasted two weeks. She tried cookery classes, as if she needed to learn anything she didn't already know, but that was all women as well.

"There's nothing wrong with women," she told her friend Sharon. They were waiting for the waiter to bring their creamy herbed wild mushroom galettes before the sun hit their table and they had to move, or the umbrella had to be shifted, or both.

"I agree," said Sharon. Definitely, in Sharon's case. She'd come out as a lesbian ten years earlier and said she'd never been happier.

"It's just … you know? I miss being hugged by somebody taller and stronger than I am. I think that's what I miss. Taller and stronger. And with hair on his arms. And his chest." She stopped, surprised at herself. "I didn't know that's what I wanted. Hair! Am I crazy? But there's a big difference." She stood up. "Where's that waiter? I could use a refill."

The waiter declined to appear. She gave up and sat again.

"The worst," she said, "was when I needed to renew my driver's licence. They asked marital status and I had to put in 'widow'."

"So you're looking for another husband," Sharon said.

"What? A what? Do you think I'm crazy? I had a great marriage, you know that. Herb and I, we were great together. I don't want another husband. Just, I don't know, I want to find a man I can go to concerts with, have a meal with, maybe a weekend in Clarens – you know, nothing serious. A meaningless, shallow relationship."

It was somewhat later, when the waiter had finally brought their galettes and she was on her second glass of chenin blanc, that Sharon brought up dating sites.

"I don't think that's for me," she said. "Is it? All kinds of weird people use those sites. And other sites. Anyway aren't they for younger people? Looking for a hook-up? Or so I'm told … And you never know what you're getting."

"There are plenty of sites for people our age," Sharon said. "And I should know. How do you think I found Bianca?"

Hours later, Esther phoned her daughter, Tessa, and mentioned she was going to look up people on the internet.

"Who are you looking for?" Tessa asked, sounding muffled. Her cellphone was cradled on her shoulder as she tried to beat sugar into chickpea liquid for a vegan meringue. It was book club in two days and she'd promised to bring something.

The phone went silent for a moment, and then Esther

explained. "I had a lot of boyfriends who wanted to marry me and I often think 'what if?'. I was 18, what did I know about marriage? I was so naïve. There was a dentist – he went on to make a lot of money. And Stanley, what was his surname? He was awfully sweet. Anyway, I thought I'd look them up."

Tessa put the meringue mixture down. "Ma, you may not find them, but you can try. Not everyone's got a profile. Or a presence. I don't, for example. Do you?"

Esther spent 10 minutes looking for herself on Google – her married name, her maiden name, various spellings. She wasn't there. But the dentist was – or, rather, his obituary.

So was the obituary for the architecture student whose proposal she'd turned down.

She remembered Stanley's surname, and she found his obituary as well. "What's going on here?" she asked the empty room.

Maybe she'd try dating sites. At least people on dating sites were, presumably, alive.

It took a while to strike up the courage, but two weeks later, Esther was sitting at her computer with her daughter, who definitely didn't need a dating site but knew her way around cyberspace.

"Okay, Ma, just put into Google what you're looking for. Do you want me to do it for you?"

"Certainly not," Esther said. "I'm sure I can do it myself." She typed in "casual relationship over 50".

"Not that specific, Ma," Tessa said. "Why don't you put in 'Dating sites for older people'?"

"I know what I want," Esther said.

"That comes later when you fill in a questionnaire."

"Oh." She wiped off "casual relationship over 50" and put in "dating sites for over 50", as instructed, and gazed rapt at the screen as ad after ad appeared.

"Look at that! There are dating sites for everybody!" She scrolled through. "Dating sites for Muslims and Jews and Christians and Catholics and gays and lesbians – I guess that's what Sharon went onto. Here's even one for Jewish gay men. Oh here we are, here's one for seniors."

"Hold on a minute, Ma. We don't know about that site. It could be …"

Too late – Esther clicked – and a naked large-breasted woman leaned out of the screen.

"Oh my God, Tessa, what is …" The woman was replaced by a naked woman with her legs spread and that was replaced by a slide show of men with men, women with women …

"Oh no oh no oh no, what do I do? How do I get this off my computer? Oh I'm panicking, I never expected …"

Tessa clicked. And then she called up the virus protector she had installed, and clicked on a total clean option.

"It's okay, Ma. The virus protector will deal with it. A lot of those sites are Trojan sites, they hook you in and install all kinds of malware. If you were a dirty old man …"

"Please, don't joke about it," Esther said. "What if a lot of weirdos start contacting me on Facebook?"

"Ma, you're not on Facebook."

"That's what I said," she said. "Thank God I'm not on Facebook. Okay, we'd better scratch that option."

"There are plenty of legitimate sites I can find for you," Tessa said.

Esther stood up. "Coffee," she said, and headed for the kitchen. Where she stood, waiting for the grounds to brew, and listed her assets. She was still attractive – she took good care of herself, and all those years on the tennis court gave her grace and fluidity. She knew how to dress well. She had a lovely house. As a retired teacher, there were many subjects she could discuss, from world politics to climate change and economics. Who wouldn't want to spend time with her?

"You're right," Sharon said as they walked at Zoo Lake a week later. "You've got to pick up the pace."

"I don't know what you mean," she said. "I'm not doing anything at the moment."

"Not pick up the pace as in finding a man. I mean let's walk a little faster. You're dawdling."

"Oh sorry." There was silence as they approached the outdoor restaurant, and relief when its smells were far behind. "So what should I do? Where does a person meet men?"

"How would I know?" They walked on. A few minutes later: "Maybe at dinner parties?"

And that was the key. Sharon phoned a couple of mutual friends, apprised them of Esther's interests, and for one Saturday night after another she was, if not the life and soul of the party, certainly a woman of interest.

She wasn't impressed by the men invited to meet her – neither the elderly advocate, nor the never-married accountant – perhaps the figures had never added up.

It was at the third dinner party that one man struck a chord. It helped that he was French, with beautiful, courtly manners, and different from everyone she knew.

And he looked lost. His wife – the sister of her hostess, Sharon's partner Bianca – had died ten years earlier. He had retired from his post teaching French at Unisa only a year before.

He phoned the day after the dinner party. The Alliance Française was having a Beaujolais Nouveau evening with jazz and wonderful hors d'oeuvres. Would she like to join him?

It was a balmy evening as they walked to the Alliance from her house, just a few streets away. Jean-Claude explained that in Paris the launch of new Beaujolais on the third

Thursday of November was a joyous ritual. It had to be drunk quickly – the grapes had been fermented for only a few weeks – and while Beaujolais was so much lighter than other red wines, for example the many types of Burgundy, Beaujolais Nouveau was lighter still, and not built to last.

By the time they reached the Alliance, Esther was hanging on every accented word. How worldly this guy was. How much he knew!

The sex came later, after a month of carefully-chosen movies – Jean-Claude was a film connoisseur – and excellent dinners at small restaurants.

They had driven in her car to the movies, and left his car safely in her garage. She pulled her BMW next to his Peugeot but before opening the passenger door he reached over, gently turned her face towards his and kissed her. "Must I leave now?" he asked.

She said the first thing that came into her head: "Please stay."

They made it as far as the living room before taking off each other's clothes.

Esther hadn't had any intention of making love, not to anyone, after her husband died. She felt it would be vaguely disloyal.

Moreover, despite the years of tennis, age and gravity had worked together, and she was, well, in some places anyway, a bit floppy.

On the other hand, so was Jean-Claude, which was more important. It took a while, but they got there.

And they kept getting there, after films, or coming back to Johannesburg after lunch in country restaurants.

"Today," Jean-Claude announced one Sunday, "I propose a trip to the Irene Market. It's not far from my home. We can pick up good bread and cheese there and of course I have some excellent Bordeaux. You have not been to my home. I will send directions."

It made sense for a Unisa lecturer to live in Pretoria, and it was only half an hour or so from Parkview. And, of course, Jean-Claude had been making the trip for more than a month. It was Esther's turn, and an easy drive on a Sunday.

The house ... it must be, she assumed, very French, with frills and frou-frous everywhere.

"My late wife," he said, "was a design genius. I relied on her taste completely."

Okay, Esther thought, that's sweet. As was the sex that followed the bread, cheese and Bordeaux.

The following Sunday she drove to Pretoria again. "There is nothing on at the cinema worth watching," he said, "but I have some excellent films I have recorded. And Esther why must you go back on Sunday? Why not stay over?"

So she packed a nightgown, a toothbrush and her moisturiser and set out for Pretoria. When she arrived she was presented with a chicken and a large Le Creuset oven roasting pot.

"I am hopeless in the kitchen," he said, "and my estimable cleaning lady has deserted me for Zimbabwe, where her daughter has just given birth. Do you think you might ..."

Of course. It was kind of sweet.

"My late wife," he said, "was a brilliant cook."

Okay, not so sweet.

The following Thursday the Johannesburg Philharmonic concert featured a visiting cellist. Esther suggested they attend. Jean-Claude begged off – he was not crazy about the programme. But would she come to Pretoria on Saturday morning and stay the weekend?

This time there was a lamb shoulder waiting for her. Worse – there was no dishwasher. And after roasting the lamb for dinner and making breakfast the next morning – although Jean-Claude did grind the beans and make the coffee – there were an awful lot of dishes.

She washed. He began drying, then decided life was too short for such a task when standing next to a beautiful woman, close enough to touch. "Shall we, perhaps, leave these dishes to dry themselves? I can think of better things to do," he said, enfolding her.

He talked her into staying another day, and then another.

He never went to the shops – he phoned various purveyors in the neighbourhood, and they delivered meat and vegetables and cases of wine.

On Tuesday they'd forgotten to send milk for the morning's café au lait, so Esther drove out to fetch it. On the way she thought about Jean-Claude's teeth. They were a bit crooked. It was something she hadn't noticed before. Why was she thinking about it now?

And why, when she returned to her Parkview house on Wednesday, was she happy to be home? She'd wanted arms to cling to. Sex was something she hadn't expected, but she could deal with it.

She'd invited Jean-Claude to that week's concert, but he hadn't liked that programme either. Nor had he been interested in going to any of the films on in Pretoria.

"I want to meet this man," her daughter said. "Will you invite him for lunch or dinner or something on the weekend?"

She did. He said he had tickets for a rugby match on Saturday and wouldn't she like to come with him? He could meet her daughter another time. "My late wife," he said, "was an expert on rugby. She knew everything about the game. The rules. The players."

Esther had no interest in rugby, which she ranked only barely above boxing matches as a brutal waste of time. So she declined and spent the weekend at home – and discovered she enjoyed it. No cooking in another woman's kitchen. No running errands for her host. She could choose what she wanted to watch on television, if she wanted to watch anything at all.

Why was he never interested in doing anything she suggested, only what he wanted to do? Was his wife really a genius in everything? When Esther mentioned her late husband, an eminent GP, Jean-Claude changed the subject.

He was so clearly wise about so many things she was not – on film, for example. And he knew so much about food. But was he really so helpless that he needed a housekeeper?

Could he really not cook? Or dry the dishes after she'd washed them, or pick up his own groceries? Or, for that matter, do his own laundry? One Monday morning she'd found herself loading a huge pile of dirty laundry into the washing machine, standing there as it went round and round, and wondering why she was doing it. Was it an automatic reaction to dirty laundry? She'd be dusting the furniture next.

His teeth became her obsession. Why had he never straightened them?

In the end, it was too much. She had not raised a family and tended a husband for 40 years to be turned into a housekeeper for a man she barely knew. And, basically, the sex had been so much better with her husband. There had been no floppiness there. She declined the next two invitations, and then he stopped phoning. She assumed his cleaning lady had returned.

"The problem is I have nothing to do, really," Esther said. "I wanted a meaningless, shallow relationship but Jean-Claude was too shallow. In fact, boring."

"Maybe you should think about bridge again," Sharon said. They were walking briskly around the Emmarentia Dam this time, trying to avoid dog poo and crazy cyclists – the usual Sunday obstacle course

"Oh no," Esther said. "I'm not going to be the kind of ageing woman who plays bridge five days a week. Oh hell," and dodged a child racing towards her on a red bicycle. "Do we have to walk here?"

"Who said five days? You don't even know how to play. Lessons. People take lessons."

"I did take lessons. I'd rather crochet. Enough of this place. Let's get coffee somewhere."

"Where? On a Sunday afternoon? You think you're in New York?"

"If only ..." she said.

§

Six months later, as she drove towards Hyde Park Corner to see what shoes were on offer – because she had very little to do these days – the car felt odd and unbalanced. She pulled into her normal service station on Jan Smuts, even though there was plenty of petrol in the tank. And sure enough, the attendant found a nail in the tyre.

She stood around while three guys jacked up the car, pulled out the nail, plugged the hole and pumped up the tyre. It gave Donald time to approach, and chat.

"You come here often, don't you?" he said, approaching. "I've seen you here often."

He was a nice-looking fellow, neatly dressed, nicely coiffed. "Only when I need petrol," she said. "Or today. Because there was an emergency."

"My car can pass anything on the road except a petrol station," he said, smiling broadly and waving towards a red F-type Jaguar. "I suppose I spend more time here than most, when I should be at my surgery."

He said he was a dentist, which made sense, she decided, looking at his perfect teeth. He told her he'd noticed her on many occasions but hadn't struck up the nerve to speak –

until today, when she seemed in some distress.

"Not really," she said. "It's being taken care of." They discussed where the tyre could have picked up the nail – anywhere on Johannesburg's filthy streets, especially with all the construction, and did they still actually use nails to hammer in, say, doors and windows? Who knew?

He moved in before the car was handed back to her. "I don't want to appear forward, but could I take you out to dinner sometime?"

Why not? "I'd like that," she said. And just like that, they decided on the Saturday night.

She knew better than to get in a car with a stranger who'd picked her up at a petrol station, so she said she'd meet him at the restaurant. He booked at a pizza/pasta chain, showing pretty awful taste for a man driving a Jaguar, but she showed up anyway, because he might have other good qualities.

"I had to Uber," he said, halfway through the meal. "The Jag packed up. I don't suppose you could drop me off home? I'm not far from here."

"Of course," she said pleasantly, already regretting the evening. Maybe it wasn't even his Jaguar. Maybe he wasn't a dentist. Maybe he was an axe murderer. She had a second glass of very ordinary merlot.

On the way to his flat, she developed a desperate urge to pee. It must have been the wine. So when he invited her in, she accepted and went straight to the bathroom, intending to do what she needed to do, and then leave.

When she walked out, he was still in the living room. Stark naked.

She didn't walk out. She ran. She didn't bother with the lift, but raced down the stairs and into her car.

A week later, as they waited for their galettes, Sharon could not stop laughing.

"It's not funny," Esther said crossly. "Now I have to change petrol stations. Do you think that's easy?"

"Bridge lessons," Sharon said. "Come on, I'll join you. We'll be unbeatable. Bianca swears by bridge."

Esther was astonished. "Bianca plays bridge?"

"What, you don't think lesbians play bridge? Are you kidding? Bridge. We'll wipe the floor with those old bats."

"Excuse me," Esther said, "I'm also an old bat. So are you."

Six months of bridge lessons later they dominated Category A at the bridge club in Oaklands and nobody wanted to play with them, except two older men who – to Esther's annoyance and Sharon's amusement – found Sharon utterly fascinating.

2

The bread takes a while to prove – or, Nothing is forever

Sophie and Jack

Julie was dying. She had been dying for a long time – long enough for her husband and daughter and friends to get used to the idea.

"I don't mind dying," she told her friend Sophie. "But what's going to happen to Jack? I don't think he'll be happy on his own."

"I'll take him," Sophie said, helpfully.

"That's okay then," Julie said, and smiled. Gratefully.

Two months later the leukemia won, leaving Jack a widower.

Sophie wasn't technically a widow, although if her partner Tommy had stayed around for another week she might have killed him, and he was still trying to steal her identity, hack into her accounts, and worm his way back into her life. Five years with an addict was long enough.

§

Two months after the funeral, Sophie and Jack went to Sun City for the weekend. No sex – it was too soon and they knew each other too well. It took Sophie many more months to make the transition from best friend of the family to part of the family, to lover, but it worked, because she'd had so much experience with difficult men.

Not that Jack was particularly difficult. Jack was everything Tommy wasn't. Start with: Normal. Caring. Honest.

And generous. So generous. Waiters could pay for a taxi home and expensive chocolates on his tips. Car guards couldn't believe their luck when he handed over a fifty.

When it came to his friends, his wife's relatives, or his daughter's friends, his generosity was more targeted. An example: Julie's nephew needed to make bail; his fifth fraud arrest carried a hefty figure. Jack wasn't worried that a sociopath like Percy would be arrested three, four, five more times before leaving the country to defraud employers and trusting comrades elsewhere – Jack just paid the bail.

A successful advocate, he had plenty of money to hand out – but so did thousands of others, whose generosity ranged from minimal to zero.

So what was he doing with a college dropout whose main accomplishment was the production of a daughter, now living 2 500 km away and learning the art of tattoo?

Sophie was what an earlier generation would have called fey, and her colleagues at the bookshop where she worked mornings and weekends considered nuts. She believed in spiders as messengers, for example, and when spotting anything smaller than a rain spider she tried to work out what it was trying to tell her.

Once, there was a spider that seemed to have shucked off its outer skin, like a snake. "Empty," she said to herself, unlocking the door of her 12-year-old Honda. "Empty. What does that mean?"

It seemed to mean there was no water in the radiator, which she discovered when smoke poured out from under the bonnet and she had to pull over on the highway and call the AA.

She also believed that dates had intrinsic meanings, that air currents carried the hopes and dreams of everyone who had ever breathed them – and maybe they did – and that her mother, who had spent her first 18 years ignoring her, was finally trying to get in touch from the Great Beyond.

That wasn't likely. Sophie's mother's main interest in her only child was to keep her out from under her feet. She'd bounced her around from one relative to another. They all had different rules, and growing up in a variety of houses Sophie never knew, for example, whether it was okay to eat a chicken or whether meat was murder, or if it was reasonable to shop on Saturdays or an offence to Hashem.

It was so confusing that Sophie, hoping for certainty in a home of her own, married the first guy who asked her. She was 18. He was violent. With a brilliant instinct for self-preservation, she walked out after explaining to him that if he thought of contesting the divorce or, in fact, ever talking to her again, she would shoot him – a skill she'd learned from the relatives she'd been placed with at 12 (and moved on from at 13).

Marriage number two, to a guy who owned a video shop, produced a daughter. And it was the daughter who brought Julie into Sophie's life.

The girls were a year apart and went to the same nursery school, and Sophie and Julie would stand around every afternoon waiting for them to race out towards the gate. It didn't occur to either of them to try a lift scheme. Their encounters, standing in the sun with other mothers, became a highlight of their day.

One day Julie mentioned she was in her church choir and Sophie perked up. "I used to sing in school," she said. She had a pure soprano voice and nowhere to use it. She was Jewish but was thrilled at the chance to sing in Julie's Anglican church choir.

"Tell me something," Julie asked one day, after Sophie was picked for a solo in "Once in Royal David's City". "Wouldn't you rather be singing in – sorry, what's it called? A synagogue? Is that right? Or something?"

"I would sing anywhere," Sophie said. "You have no idea how much this means to me."

Sophie hadn't had much of a life. She'd left husband number two after finding him in bed one day with another man. She cried, he cried, they agreed to part. She had scooped up her daughter, driven from Durban to Johannesburg, rented a flat and found an inexpensive divorce lawyer and a part-time job in a bookshop. Husband number two had barely enough money to support himself, let alone Sophie and their daughter.

She had wanted to be a teacher but the teacher training colleges had been scrapped, and on her own there wasn't enough money for university.

She wasn't ready to give up – she'd found a private college that could train her as a nursery school teacher for a reduced fee if she'd spend two mornings a week answering their phone. That lasted several months, until one day the CEO stuck his hand up her dress while she was explaining the course to a caller and she slammed the receiver into his crotch, followed by an elbow into his ample gut.

Julie had been a teacher before she'd had her daughter. "You're so lucky," Sophie said. "I always wanted to be a teacher. I guess I never will now."

"I was pretty good at it too," Julie said. "I think. But I don't know. Jack thinks wives belong at home. He's strange."

Jack grew up in a village 50km from Bloemfontein. His mother had two daughters before she hit the jackpot with a son. She had never worked. Why should she? She was always there for him, if not always for his sisters.

His father was full of praise for the woman he'd had the good sense to marry. She rose well before dawn, up to her elbows kneading bread dough – Jack had never tasted store-bought bread until he went to boarding school – or grinding chunks of meat for hamburgers, or sizzling mutton for the stew the family would be having for dinner. She baked wonderful cakes, and decorated them beautifully.

"And me? I'm pretty good at boiling an egg," Julie said. "That's about it. Although you do have to watch it."

Jack's mother made sure he went to the best boarding school in the Free State and, later, to university in Johannesburg, where he met Julie.

Teachers in those days were trained on a different campus, but Julie had become friendly with one of Jack's sisters, also training as a teacher, and one day Madeleine had taken her along to Jack's digs to fetch a book.

It was a happy marriage. Jack forgave Julie's lack of culinary skill. He loved everything else about her – her warmth, her beauty, and her devotion to their daughter, for she had stopped teaching when Ruth was born.

It was his view that all marriages should be like the marriage of his parents, who shared everything. If Jack wanted to watch a film, or a television programme, or a play, or a rugby match, he expected Julie to join him. When friends came over to play cards, he expected Julie to play hostess.

There was no sharing in chambers – Jack was an advocate, not an attorney, so he worked alone. Julie listened when he discussed details of the cases he was handling, although her eyes tended to glaze over; fortunately, there was no quiz afterwards. It was basically a one-way street: Julie didn't talk about her day. She listened, and shared his ups and downs.

And then, 20 years into the marriage, Julie got sick. And two years later, she died.

Sophie took charge of the wake and showed up every afternoon for the first week to make sure Jack and Ruth were okay. Her presence was not unusual – she and Julie had been so close that Jack was okay with Julie travelling on choir tours without him as long as Sophie was with her to handle any problems.

Julie had had a word with Jack before she died, explaining that she would not be leaving him alone. "Don't talk about it," he'd said. "Life without you ..." and then he'd started to weep, and the subject was dropped.

But he'd always been fond of Sophie, as strange as she was. Where Julie was soft and pliable, Sophie was tough, with rough edges. Jack had been raised as a fine specimen of Free State manhood. Women were fragile and should stay at home, as his mother did. Yet Sophie looked after herself, out in the world. She even drove around the city at night. Jack had forbidden Julie to endanger herself by driving alone after dark; if she needed to go somewhere, they would go together.

Ruth became engaged while Jack and Sophie were at Sun City, and when they returned to Johannesburg it was Sophie whom Ruth turned to for advice. Together they examined venues, decided on dates, looked at gowns, wrote the guest list. All Jack had to do was write the cheques.

"You will stand up with me at the reception, won't you?" Ruth asked Sophie.

"Will they allow it?" Sophie asked. "I'm not your mother."

"You're in loco parentis," Ruth said. "Anyway, if you're there, I know my mom will be there too."

The wedding was held in St Francis's Anglican Church on Tyrone Avenue, not far from the flat Ruth and her now-husband had rented. The pews were packed, and the wedding photographs in the garden turned out very well. Ruth insisted that Sophie be in the pictures, standing next to Jack.

§

Jack and Sophie waited until after the wedding to move in together.

It did not go smoothly.

There was Sophie's refusal to give up her bookshop job (because life is uncertain) and her devotion to *The Bold and the Beautiful*, which Jack found both inexplicable and idiotic.

Then there was the day she carefully carried a rain spider into the garden instead of killing it. "You never know," she told Jack. "Maybe he's trying to tell us something. Let me think ... he was suspended over the stove ..."

The strangeness Jack had found charming when he only had to deal with it now and then became intensely irritating when he was living with it.

But there was an upside. Sophie found the details of his cases fascinating – she even ventured the odd intelligent comment. She was happy to let Jack choose movies, and although she would normally have moved to another city rather than watch rugby from the stands at Ellis Park, she dutifully went along and showed enthusiasm, if not much knowledge.

For Sophie had found what she'd been looking for all her life – like the song, someone to watch over her, while she was watching over him.

The housekeeper Jack had hired for her cooking skills retired after the wedding to the small house that, characteristically, he had paid for and furnished. Sophie meanwhile had always nurtured a deep, secret desire to be a domestic goddess. At last, this was her chance to try.

She began by poring over the cookery books in the bookshop when there were no customers needing her attention. She copied some of the more complicated recipes to try out when she could source ingredients like molasses vinegar, celeriac and squid. Then she began watching cooking programmes while Jack was at work or in court – she took notes and tried out the simpler recipes. Very few of them worked.

Finally, she went online to find cookery classes. One Tuesday evening she found herself whipping up a cheesecake – the class was, fortuitously, scheduled for Jack's poker night at the house of another card player.

"Do you find this difficult?" she asked the woman she was paired with.

"Not really," said the woman, whose name was Esther. "I already know how to cook. I've made this hundreds of times. I was just bored. And hoping to meet someone interesting here. But ... no."

Sophie didn't take that personally. But she did want to know how to make something more challenging than cheesecake.

"Scones?" said the teacher, when Sophie asked her after class.

"Bread," said Sophie. "Vol au vent. Slow-cooked lamb shoulder with mint and cumin. Monkfish tagine with mussels and ras el hanout. But mostly I want to know how to make bread."

There was something about Sophie's determination that struck a spark. "You could go to a demonstration I'm giving on Saturday morning," she said, "but bread is not on the menu. Can you get to Morningside on Saturday afternoon?"

"Probably not," Sophie admitted. "My partner likes to watch sports on Saturday afternoons and he wants me there. I can come any weekday afternoon, though."

"Perfect," said the teacher. "Tuesday afternoon, around one. You'll have to pay for the ingredients, and a small fee for the teaching. And bread takes time – you'd better come back on Wednesday."

Sophie learned a lot during her two months of private lessons. Money for increasingly expensive ingredients wasn't a problem – she used her wages from the bookshop so that Jack wouldn't know what she was up to. She wanted to surprise him.

Finally, she was ready.

One summer morning, Jack was awakened at 5am by the sun pouring in through blinds they had forgotten to close the night before. He reached over and found Sophie's side of the bed empty, so he went in search of her.

He found her in the kitchen, up to her elbows kneading dough, a stew bubbling on the stove.

"I thought it would be a good idea to start dinner before I have to leave for the bookshop," she said. "And the bread can prove while I'm ... Whoo, hold on. If you're going to grab me like that let me get the dough off my hands."

And so it continued, for 20 years. Every so often, Jack would suggest Sophie quit her job at the bookshop – and she'd counter with a coq au vin, or a pad thai, or – once – a beef Wellington, to prove she could do it all, and that her job did not interfere with her life at home.

And then Jack had a heart attack – not the result of all that good food, but a genetic predisposition. The next day, Jack's lawyer handed Sophie an envelope marked In the Event of My Death. The note inside assured her that the funeral had been booked and paid for, and directed her to the funeral home he'd chosen.

"It was a very bizarre experience," said the young woman behind the counter. "He came in one day, it must have been – wait, I have it here. It was exactly two years ago next month. And he said 'I would like to arrange a funeral.' Well this is a family firm, I grew up here, I thought I'd seen it all. But when I asked who's it for and he said 'For me' ... Oh sorry, you must be feeling terrible."

"I am, actually," Sophie said. "But Jack always wanted to be in control. You know? So I'm not really surprised."

"He picked out a coffin, told us where he'd bought a plot

– next to his first wife ..."

"His only wife," Sophie said.

"Yes, well ... anyway, and he paid for everything. Quite an expensive coffin. He even chose the flowers. There's a wreath of white roses from you and red roses from his daughter."

Jack would have been glad but not surprised that the funeral went off without a hitch, and the wake afterwards – which he'd also arranged and paid for – was a great success.

It was something for Sophie to remember when she whipped up gourmet suppers in her one-bedroom flat. Jack had left the house, the cars and most of his money to his daughter. He'd left Sophie a few shares that paid reasonable dividends, but she was hardly going to spend it all on expensive accommodation.

Is it possible to shrug while you're packing? She did. Because it was lovely while it lasted – "Wasn't it, Tiger?" she said often to her cat, who had gone with her to the new flat – and "Nothing is forever". Except, perhaps, her job in the bookshop, still going strong.

3

Alone

Thandeka

Thandeka had a bad feeling about the whole affair.

"Don't go. I don't see why it has to be you again," she said. "Why is it always you?"

"I have the bigger car," Kagiso said reasonably. "Anyway, Kabelo's gone to watch football."

"Hasn't anybody in your family heard of Uber?"

"Probably not. Look, I'll be back by eight. Just hold dinner."

He wasn't back by eight. The next morning, when Thandeka returned home after driving her daughter to school, police were waiting for her. There had been a pileup on the highway, they said, she might have heard about it on the news, and her husband, his sister and his mother were among the casualties.

She looked at the policemen – a man and a woman – but appeared not to see them.

"Did you hear what I said?" the man asked.

She stood there, silent and unseeing, for another long minute. Then "Thank you," she said. "You can go now."

"You can't be alone," the policewoman said.

"I won't be," she said, and phoned her mother.

An hour later, the lounge was full of people. Her uncle Langa's wife Mmatuna went into the bedroom and working together, slowly, she and Thandeka managed to pull the heavy mattress off the bed and shove it against the wall, still covered with a light blue fitted sheet.

Thandeka wrapped a doek around her weave and a blanket from her daughter Thuli's room around her shoulders – it had characters from Frozen on it, but the alternative was Spiderman, whom her daughter had fallen in love with the year before.

Except for the phone call to her mother, asking her to fetch Thuli after school and keep her in the family home in Sandton, Thandeka had not spoken a word. Nor had she cried. What was the point?

Once ensconced on the mattress, she was truly alone. Mmatuna was busy in the kitchen, making tea and snacks for the visitors. Her uncle Langa was outside, making sure nobody parked on the pavement.

But she wasn't alone for long. When her neighbours across the road saw the commotion they came out to ask what was going on, and when they were told, they came in to help. Sharon cried enough tears for both of them, kneeling by the mattress, holding Thandeka's hands, while Bianca helped carry the cups in and out of the kitchen. Thandeka's sister Nompilo arrived after work and joined her on the mattress, and her mother came shortly afterwards, having left Thuli with her grandfather.

It was only when Kagiso's brother Kabelo showed up that Thandeka spoke, and all she said was "Where were you?"

He didn't answer, and then he left.

He returned the next day. Pulling a chair over to the mattress, he told Thandeka that his brother, his mother and his sister would be buried in the ancestral village in North West. "Do what you like with your mother and sister," Thandeka said. "Kagiso will be buried in Johannesburg."

"He is my brother," Kabelo said. "I will decide."

"He was my husband," Thandeka said. "Basically, it's up to me."

Mmatuna backed her up. "Watch that one," she said.

32

"This is the 21st century, not the 19th. And we're in Johannesburg, not – where's his family from? Taung. I don't think he realises. And by the way, I'm proud of you. I know you have no interest in tradition, but you're doing well."

Later that day Thandeka had a call from the funeral home, confirming the order to ship all three bodies to North West.

"No!" she shouted, and started to get up off the mattress.

"You can't go," said her scandalised aunt. "We will handle it."

"Give me a minute to get dressed. That damned mattress is wrecking my back."

Mmatuna followed her into the bedroom.

"At least wear black," she said. "And cover your head."

In the end, Thandeka was accompanied by Mmatuna, Nompilo and her uncle Langa, standing in for her father, who needed to be at the office, and her mother, who was still looking after Thuli.

Langa turned onto the Golden Highway. "Where are you taking us?" Thandeka asked.

"Black bodies go to black undertakers," he said.

"Not one of those fly-by-nights with a few freezers in the garage?"

Langa winced. "We will move him."

But they didn't have to. The premises were muted and welcoming, the funeral home large, with many rooms, and the staff suitably subdued. Thandeka, kitted out in a black two-piece outfit, black stockings and a crisp black headdress, explained to the funeral director that she was the wife – as if that needed an explanation – and under no circumstances was her late husband to go anywhere but West Park.

"Not Avalon? There are excellent facilities at Avalon," said the director.

"West Park," she said firmly. "My daughter and I live not far away and we must be able to visit my late husband's grave as often as we can."

"Of course," said the director. He turned to Langa. "We must make arrangements for the funeral. And there are other matters ... the coffin, flowers, transport –"

Thandeka interrupted. "May I see my husband?"

"Of course," said the director. "Understand, he has been laid out in a temporary coffin. It is very plain."

Kagiso looked serene, and beautiful. Thandeka had to steady herself. She held onto the table holding the temporary coffin, and then she fainted.

The funeral happened a week later. On the following Monday, Thandeka and her sister tried to return the mattress to the bed it had come from, but it was too heavy. Thandeka called her neighbour, who lent a hand, then left, saying she had soup on the stove.

"It's pretty soon, but I can understand why you want to move on," Nompila said.

"I've been away long enough. I have to go to work. Tomorrow." Thandeka hadn't used up her compassionate leave from Wits University, where she had a major-time post teaching architecture to the third years, but she needed to get moving.

"Remember when Oupa died? Mama spent six months sitting at home. No music, no movies, not even a meal out."

"I will mourn Kagiso for the rest of my life," Thandeka said. "Just not the way I'm told to mourn."

"So no cleansing ceremony?"

"I don't know. I'll worry about that when I have a moment. Which is not now."

"Okay. Can I drive you to work? Should I fetch Thuli from Mama?"

"Oh, yes, please fetch Thuli tomorrow, thanks. That would be helpful. Poor Mama, she hasn't had a life since ..." She trailed off.

On Tuesday morning, Thandeka donned her black outfit

because she felt it would honour Kagiso. She stood by her car, neglected in the carport, its battery draining, then turned away. It was too soon. Instead she walked two blocks to Lower Park Drive and along Zoo Lake to the taxis parked near Jan Smuts Avenue.

"The students were very kind," she told Nompilo that afternoon. "They didn't know where to look but they tried to be supportive. Especially Emily. You know Emily, I've spoken about her. The girl from Nigeria. She has brilliant ideas and the others, they laugh at her. All the time. We're doing an amazing project on a migration centre, and Emily has the best ideas. Well, I suppose she would have. That part was all right. But taking a taxi, that was not the best idea I've ever had. You cannot believe … I'd heard stories, but …"

"Oh no. Oh no, Thandeka."

"I had the back seat to myself. No-one wanted to be anywhere near me," she said. "Both ways." She'd taken off the headdress for the return trip, but somehow, people knew. "Do they think if they sit near me I'll bring them bad luck? Are they crazy?"

"I'll drive you in tomorrow. And pick you up."

"We'll see," she said.

Thandeka and Thuli talked long into the night about Kagiso. Losing a father was a lot for a seven-year-old to grasp. Thandeka fell back on religion, but Thuli was not impressed by knowing that her father was with Jesus and not with her.

"I can see your point, darling," she said. "But it's not up to us."

Thuli curled up next to Thandeka, who finally fell asleep sometime before dawn.

Nompilo was waiting outside as Thandeka finished packing Thuli's lunchbox. "I'll come back for you," she said, as Thuli climbed into the BMW.

"I have to try," Thandeka said. "Let me try. But please, can you pick Thuli up? In case I don't make it."

Nompilo gave her a look, then pulled away.

Thandeka made it just in time – another day and she would have had to call the AA to charge the battery.

When she came home there was a van parked in the driveway with North West licence plates.

Inside, she was confronted by her brother-in-law and two men she had never seen before.

"How did you get in here?" she asked angrily.

"Why are you gallivanting around the city?" Kabelo said. "Are you already looking for a new husband?"

"I have a job and a child to support," she said. "And I don't have to answer to you. What do you want?"

"This is no longer your house," he said.

"Kabelo," she said calmly, "the world has moved on. You and your father have no right to my house."

One of the men spoke up. "The father and brother of the deceased are the natural heirs. You are only a woman."

"I am a woman whose name is on the deed," she said. "You can all leave now."

"Prove it," said the man.

"I don't have to prove anything to you. Now get out of my house. Out! Out!" She was shouting. "Get out!"

As the van moved away, she phoned a locksmith and by nightfall the locks had been changed.

It didn't help. The next afternoon, the security company phoned to tell her that her house had been broken into. They said they had tried her husband's number but there had been no answer, and her cellphone had been the backup. "He died two weeks ago," she told the ADT operator. "Just call me in future." Then she headed for home.

The lock had been torn from the door and anything

moveable and possibly valuable had gone – the television set, Thuli's kid's laptop, her iPad, the DStv decoder, Kagiso's lovingly tended turntable, the speakers and his collection of vinyl 78s. The filing cabinet in the study had been emptied out – clearly these were not thieves. She found the title deed torn into pieces and briefly had to smile, if bitterly. Kagiso had insisted they keep the original in a safety deposit box. His brother and thuggish confederates had only found a photocopy.

She phoned her mother. "I'm going to the police, Mama," she said. "He can't get away with this."

"Leave it," her mother said. "You'll only make it worse. And you can't prove it was Kabelo."

"Why will the police make it worse?"

"You have to go to the police, for the insurance. I assume Kagiso took out insurance? I know you never think of anything practical. Just don't say it was Kabelo."

"Why not? I know who it was."

"Don't you know why he did it?"

Thandeka sighed. "Some ancient misogynistic tradition where I'm property," she said. "Useful for breeding. Overtaken by the Constitution. Also he hates me. Always has."

"That's true, I suppose. You two have never gotten along. I think you're too … too modern for Kabelo."

There was a pause. "Mama? Are you still there?"

She was. "Thandeka," she said, "there are places the Constitution doesn't matter."

"Parkview isn't one of them," Thandeka said.

"Be thankful you're here in Johannesburg. I know a woman in Mamelodi who lost her husband and then her house. There are children in Mamelodi living alone in shacks because their parents died and their uncle took over the house and threw them out. You know, maybe you don't know, I go up there once a month to pack food parcels for the little ones. The church looks after them as best it can."

"I had no idea." She was silent for a moment, then took a deep breath. "Listen, I'm going to nail that bastard."

"Wait a minute. Thandeka, he didn't do it out of malice. He did it out of guilt. He feels it was his fault Kagiso died. Can't you see that?"

She couldn't see the connection. But when her father phoned and told her under no circumstances was she to implicate Kabelo, or it would never end, she gave in. She was smart and angry but she was also a dutiful daughter.

The police duly took down the list of items removed, and she submitted the case number to the insurance company – she had found the policy while sorting out the mess of papers in the study. ADT phoned to tell her that for a year she would not be billed, a service offered to women who had lost their husbands.

That's when she wept.

The next two weeks were a sleepwalk. She rose in the morning, packed Thuli's lunchbox, dropped her off on the way to work, picked her up in the afternoon, cooked dinner, put her child to bed, tried to read.

Food became a problem. Whatever she ate made her stomach hurt, and in any case she would not be able to keep it down. So she stopped eating, subsisting largely on tea and, in the morning, a piece of dry toast.

Then she stopped sleeping. Kagiso had often had difficulty falling asleep, and when that happened, he took sleeping tablets. She rummaged through the top drawer of his dresser, pitching out half-used blister packs of Rennies, anti-itch cream, a nail clipper, a battery tester, a spare cellphone and charger, a medical mask he used when he mowed the lawn. The sleeping tablets were in a box from the chemist – no name, no package insert, no instructions. It didn't matter. She'd seen him take them often enough.

So on the second night with no sleep, she took a tablet.

It didn't work.

She got up, checked on Thuli, drank a glass of water, went back to bed.

Then she took another two, to be sure.

She woke up in a room full of people, with somebody holding her up, making her walk. Uh oh – it was her father.

"What did you think you were doing?" he said.

"I just wanted to get some sleep," she managed.

Thuli had banged on the door and then on Thandeka, and when that hadn't roused her, she'd run across the road in her pajamas and banged on Sharon's door.

Sharon had raced over, called Thandeka's parents and started shaking her, screaming at her. Thandeka vaguely remembered hearing a screeching sound and feeling the earth shake. By the time her parents arrived, she was on the edge of consciousness, and in a way she regretted that.

"What if Thuli hadn't found you?" her mother said. "What if she'd found you too late?"

"Could you live with that?" Sharon said.

Even in her dozy state, Thandeka realised that made no sense. "That makes no sense," she said. Or thought she said.

"My aunt Muriel tried to kill herself," Sharon said. "We were devastated … She made notes on how to …"

"I just wanted to get some sleep," Thandeka said, but nobody was listening – they were too busy shouting at her. All but Thuli, who hugged her around the knees.

It was a turning point. Her mother made scrambled eggs and bacon and she kept it down. The next day when Thuli asked for KFC she obliged, and as Thuli wolfed down a drumstick and a thigh – plus chips – it all smelled so wonderful that Thandeka, who thought she'd settle for a wing or two, went for the second drumstick.

A week later Thuli asked her what the circle was on the

calendar in the kitchen.

Thandeka took a deep breath. "That was your daddy's birthday," she said. "We were going to go somewhere special."

"Where, Mama?"

"I don't know, darling."

"I know. Zoo Lake Park!" Thuli talked about the time her father had tried to teach her how to kick the ball better than the boys could.

"And can you?"

"Umm. Sometimes. You know what? When we went to where Daddy is from?"

"Taung," Thandeka said.

"And he told me about how the whole town is in a creature?"

"That's a crater, darling. A big hole in the ground."

"Crater. Because a meteor fell down from the sky? And when Daddy took me to where he works? And then we had ice cream? And when Daddy showed me how to ride a bicycle and I didn't fall down? Mama, do you think …"

"What, darling?"

"Do you think he's watching us? Can we have a birthday party for Daddy? Even if he's in heaven with Jesus?"

On Kagiso's birthday, that's exactly what they did. Thandeka packed a picnic lunch with Kagiso's favourite sandwiches – cold boerewors – and they set out for Zoo Lake, where Thuli showed the little boys playing soccer that she could kick the ball just as well as they could.

Watching her child send the ball past the goalkeeper, Thandeka smiled, for the first time in weeks.

4

The housing crisis

Charlotte

It was a small cul-de-sac, with four houses, each owned and occupied by a woman living alone. Dierdre had thrown her husband out after finding him with her sister. Jacky's husband, crossing the park one night looking for a rent boy, had stumbled into the lake and drowned. Joan's husband had shot himself when he thought his business was failing.

Shereen had never married. She was pleased about that – as a GP, she made enough money on her own, and when she thought of her neighbours' husbands, she was glad she'd never committed to any of the men she'd been involved with.

Then there was Charlotte.

Charlotte lived around the corner. A graphic artist with a studio in the cottage behind the house, she'd married an estate agent and set about having a family.

Their daughter Lianne was only five when Charles died.

Their son Ian was six days old.

When Charles visited Charlotte and his new son at the Park Lane she'd noticed how tired he looked. But he was a strong, athletic man – tennis every weekend, squash and gym when he could fit it in. He assured her it was nothing, that he'd not been sleeping well but as soon as she was back it would all come right.

She'd been home from the hospital for a few days when Charles came back from gym, showered and changed. He'd settled in front of the television to check the news when she heard him say "Oh my God something's wrong!"

She raced out of the kitchen. His face was white. "Get Shereen!" he managed to say before passing out.

Shereen shooed Charlotte back into the kitchen and called an ambulance. It was, she was told later, an aneurysm, and Charles died on the way to the hospital.

So there she was: widowed at 30, with a skill that, while valued, didn't pull in much money, a bond to pay, food to buy ... and a newborn baby to tend to.

Charles's brother David, his closest friend Brian and a mutual friend, Laurence, who ran a financial services operation, called a meeting in her living room a few days later.

"We have to consider that you can't keep living in this big house," David said by way of an opening remark.

"Excuse me?" Charlotte said.

"How are you going to pay for it? The family will help out, but ..."

Brian broke in. "What David is trying to say ... what's the bond on this house?"

"High," Charlotte said. "But I can't think about it now. I'm in a very dark place."

"Did Charles leave insurance? Do you have investments you can cash in? Do you know which clients he was working with, what's still to be wound up?"

"I don't know. I can't think about it. I'd better feed the baby."

That's when Laurence spoke. "Before you go, Charlotte, here's something practical you can do. The bank doesn't know that Charles has died. I assume you have signing rights on his account?" She nodded. "Good. Go to the bank tomorrow and withdraw as much money as possible before the bank freezes the account. You'll need it to live on until you decide what to do."

Practical advice appealed to Charlotte. It was something

to focus on in the short term, a task she could actually carry out after she'd dropped Lianne off at play school.

So on Monday, Charlotte went along to the bank and discovered there was not a lot of money in Charles's bank account. There was enough to live on for perhaps three months, if she was very careful. But the business was relatively new. Charles had gone out on his own after years working for other people, and most of the money had been used to cover expenses. Her route was clear: she would have to keep the business going.

Only one problem: she knew practically nothing about real estate. She'd answered the phone on occasion, taken messages, downloaded the odd contract, even helped to put pointer boards out at 6.30 on Sunday mornings, but there her involvement had ended. Charles had tried to involve her in case, as he put it, something happened, but she hadn't been all that interested.

Now she was interested, and there was a name that rang a bell: Tony van Deventer, a sort of unofficial partner – Charles and Tony often worked together. She'd met him only once, at the funeral. Back home from the bank, she found his number on Charles's phone.

'So sorry,' he said, when she identified herself. "A real tragedy. What can I do for you?"

She explained. He was silent, finally said "I don't know…"

"I'd be a real asset," Charlotte said. "Charles relied on me for many things."

"Look, let's meet somewhere and talk about it. How about Thursday?"

By Thursday she'd looked up the requirements for becoming an estate agent. There were two routes: a year-long internship, or a combination of an internship and a six-month course, which she could take online through Unisa. Both would lead to certification, and both were possible, although the Unisa course materials could be expensive.

Her wardrobe wasn't a problem – she'd chosen a suit to look professional.

But babysitting was. She was putting on her lipstick when her helper reminded her it was Thursday afternoon, her half-day off, and she had an arrangement.

"But I have an appointment," Charlotte said.

"And I also have somewhere I have to be," said her helper.

There was no way around it. Charlotte loaded Ian, his bottle and his blanket into the car and made it to Tony's office on time.

Tony was not charmed at the sight of a grieving widow and her newborn son.

"I don't really need an intern," he said. "Don't you think you should concentrate on being a mother?"

"If I had an option," Charlotte said, trying to be calm, "do you think my choice would be sitting in your office negotiating an internship? You won't be sorry. Give me a chance. You won't regret it."

Tony looked unconvinced. Mostly, he looked uneasily at Ian, who was sleeping.

She plunged in. "For one thing," she said, "I'm really good at canvassing."

She wasn't bad at negotiating, either. Laurence had given her the only bit of sensible advice anyone had offered since Charles's death, so she phoned him the day before her interview to ask the best way to proceed. He said that as an intern in a business that operated via commissions she wouldn't qualify for a salary, but she could offer Tony the lion's share of a commission for … what? What could she do?

"Not a lot," she said. "I don't know anything."

"He doesn't know that. Let's think strategically. What do estate agents hate to do?"

She tried to remember what Charles complained about the most. "I've got it," she said finally. "Charles disliked show houses. You know, wasting a Sunday afternoon guarding the place while chancers looked around to see what they could steal. But he really hated canvassing. That's phoning people at dinnertime asking if they want to sell their houses."

"It sounds like something that will destroy your soul," Laurence said. "What else didn't he like?"

"He didn't like distributing mail drops in new areas," she said, remembering Charles complaining about barking dogs and gates without doorbells.

"Offer that then," Laurence said. "And tell Tony you'll only take 40% of any sale arising from one of your calls. He won't agree to that but don't go lower than 20%. You can also volunteer for show house duty, by the way, but only if he pays you."

In the end, she agreed to 18% but she didn't tell Laurence. What she did tell Laurence about, however, was the Parkview house Tony and Charles had been working on together. She vaguely remembered Charles talking about it, how it was overpriced and nobody was likely to make an offer unless the owners came down by at least a million.

Laurence said it was her trump card – she should tell Tony she would take over Charles's half of the deal, and help to sell it. Tony would never agree, but he might begin to take her seriously.

There were probably other deals Charles had made with Tony, ones he hoped she didn't know about – because as soon as she mentioned the Parkview house and offered to share the proceeds, he quickly agreed to take her on as his intern – and then restricted her to a completely different neighbourhood.

She'd never heard of the area. "Buy a map," he said.

On Friday, she drove around the area he'd assigned to her

– a slightly rundown suburb with small houses and unkempt front gardens, at least the ones she could see through the gates.

She had calling cards printed and a week later, she drove back to the neighbourhood and put the cards in every mailbox or, when there was no mailbox, wedged into the security gate.

When two days passed and no one had responded, she began ringing doorbells. Even in this modest neighbourhood, it was the domestic helper who peered out of the front door and said the madam wasn't at home, she should come back later. And those were the good calls.

Mostly there were gates with no bells, or houses where she could see someone inside but nobody came out – only the dogs seemed interested in greeting her, loudly and enthusiastically.

It was discouraging, the day was hot, and when she walked into her own house, she flopped down on the day bed next to Ian's cot and wondered what it would be like, concentrating again on being a mother. When Lianne was born, that's what she'd done.

She could easily steal a few hours away from the baby to work in the cottage. She had a reputation, she was fast, intelligent and gifted. But graphic designers did not make a great deal of money. She had a bond to pay and two children to feed.

Ian took that moment to remind her that he was very hungry, and if she didn't do something about it, he would scream the house down. Lianne had been a good baby, sunny, happy, and undemanding. Ian was the opposite. Maybe baby boys were different?

As she plugged him to her breast the phone rang.

It sounded like an elderly woman. "You the estate agent?" she asked.

"I am," she said, juggling baby and phone and trying to drop neither.

"Come see me," she said. "I think I have to get out of this place."

Another hand would have been helpful. Charlotte mumbled the address, the woman's name and the day and time over and over: Smit. 34. Monday. Two. Smit. 34. Monday. Two – until she reached the whiteboard she had optimistically installed in the nursery, grabbed a koki pen, and wrote it all down.

Tony asked her to sit in a show house on Sunday just a few streets away from where she lived, take down the names of interested people and hand out his cards and an information sheet. "It's possible no one will come," he told her. "It's been on the market for a year. The owners refuse to come down on price. Everyone thinks their own house is a mansion."

Okay, not a mansion, Charlotte thought. But quite a lot of house, wonderful oak floors, beautiful high ceilings, and the garden ... paradise. At 6.30 a.m. on Sunday she and Lianne – who thought it an exciting new game – were out putting For Sale and This Way boards on the street. Ian was in the car, happily asleep.

The house was on show that afternoon from 2 to 5, and her helper, forewarned, agreed to come back early to look after the children.

Charlotte was beyond grateful. But as she was leaving, Ian began to cry, and refused to stop. Nothing would soothe him, not Felicity's back, nor a cuddle from his adored older sister. It had to be Charlotte.

"Uh oh," she said, but picked him up, along with his nappy bag, and took him along.

Despite Tony's pessimistic prediction, people did show up. First came a twenty-something couple, the woman very pregnant, the man looking as if he'd been dragged there. As

Charlotte and the woman cooed over Ian, the man picked up one of Tony's info sheets about the house and said, "I can't believe the price."

"Nor can we," Charlotte said. "It's been on the market for a year. I think by now, the owners may be open to negotiation."

Where did that come from? "There's a sizeable cottage in the back, by the way," she added. "Good for an AirBnB. Or a nanny. Or a studio."

The woman smiled at Charlotte gratefully, and the couple disappeared into the kitchen, then out the back.

Shortly afterwards, an older man on his own came and went within ten minutes, and didn't take a flyer. He was followed by another couple who looked to be at an age to downsize, not take on a big house with a garden and a cottage. Two women, fifty-something, arrived and cooed at Ian, who seemed to be enjoying the attention.

"So what do you think, Bianca?" one of the women asked her companion.

"Too big," she replied. "Anyway, we have a house. Why are we here again?"

"We like to check out the neighbourhood," she said, and turned to Charlotte. "I saw there was a show day and didn't want Tony to sit here all day for nothing. But you're not Tony."

"Clearly," Charlotte said. "Do you stay around here?"

"We do. Not far. On the next street. I haven't seen you before. Are you working for Tony?"

"I'm an intern. I don't really know anything."

"Tony's good. You'll learn a lot. Come on, Bianca, let's see who's stealing the silver."

"They must have locked it up," Bianca said.

"Who knows?" she said, and they went into the lounge.

It occurred to Charlotte that she should be checking on

the visitors, so she put Ian over her shoulder and marched into the garden – where she found the older couple digging up irises.

"Would you mind," she asked, "putting those back?"

The woman looked embarrassed, but her husband didn't bat an eye. "They have more than they need," he said. "They'll never miss a few. At this time of our lives ..."

"Just please put them back," Charlotte said. "You'll get me fired."

"I think we should, John," said the woman. "See, she can't even afford a nanny. Has to bring the baby to work."

He looked at the baby, drooling on her shoulder. "I suppose you need the money," he said grumpily. "Here." He thrust the iris bulbs, close to blooming, at her unencumbered hand and he and his wife walked out.

Charlotte put the bulbs down – how was she supposed to replant them, with a baby on her shoulder? – and turned to go back. That's when she noticed a gap among the roses, and remembered the size of the woman's handbag. Ian would fit in there, she thought.

She was back at her post in the entrance when Bianca and her friend came back. She told them about the plants.

"You've got to be on your toes," said Bianca's partner. "I'm Sharon, by the way. You should come for coffee one day. Bring the baby. He's very sweet."

Hard on their heels came the young couple. The husband seemed very enthusiastic. "The cottage would make a brilliant office," he said. "I can't continue working in the house when the baby comes. The noise alone ..."

He looked at Ian. Ian looked back. Well, in his general direction.

At last it was five, and Charlotte could lock up, put the boards back in her car and go home.

Tony phoned her the next morning to say a bid had come

through. "They're offering a lot less," he said, "but I'll sound out the owners. It depends on how keen they are to get rid of the place."

The bidders turned out to be the young couple. "We haven't had any bids for months," Tony said. "What did you say to them?"

"Not much," she said. "I did tell them about the cottage though. There are so many things you can do with a cottage. I work in mine."

"You know," Tony said, "you just may be good at this."

But Charlotte knew: if there was a sale, it was all due to Ian, who – by his very presence – had reminded the man that he'd need somewhere to work besides his lounge, or wherever he was set up, once the baby arrived.

§

On Monday afternoon just before two o'clock she was standing in front of a heavy door, stained mahogany, polished and set into a three-metre concrete wall. Mrs Smit lived in a semi-detached house and the contrast with its twin was stark – the wall next door was stained and filthy and the paint was peeling off the door. Neither gate had a bell, so she phoned.

The woman who came to the street door had to be at least seventy, despite the chestnut hair tied back, the jeans, the heels.

"Belinda," she said, holding out her hand. "You're the estate agent who can sell this place. Maybe you can work miracles. Can I offer you a cup of tea? Maybe you'd prefer coffee? Heaven knows I do."

"Coffee would be lovely, thanks." There were steps up to the front door, polished red within an inch of their lives – they glowed, something Charlotte had not thought possible.

Inside it was clean, recently painted, and much larger than

she expected. She wandered through the bedrooms, the separate dining room, glanced out the back at a garden.

"Ja, I've lived here for more than thirty years," Belinda said, carrying a tray into the lounge. She poured the coffee, offered sugar – "Why not?" Charlotte said – and milk, which was declined.

"We raised our family here, Errol and I. And it wasn't a bed of flowers, I can tell you that. In the beginning there were stones thrown on the roof. Every night. Once they threw a brick through the window – that one there" – she pointed. "It just missed Errol."

"But?" Charlotte asked. "What was their problem? Thirty years ago? The group areas act was gone ..."

"They still didn't want a coloured family living here, you see. But we had no choice. We weren't going to raise our sons where the gangs ran wild. Westbury? Bosmont? The gangs were in the schools, they were everywhere. What's a stone on the roof compared to that?"

"It's a lovely house," Charlotte said. "Pressed ceilings, beautiful hardwood floors, the original fireplace surround, a lovely garden."

"It didn't look lovely when we moved in. That fireplace had seven layers of paint. The floors were covered with a filthy carpet, and the garden – you wouldn't believe it. Like a jungle. Like the bush."

"You've done a beautiful job. Why do you want to sell? Surely nobody's throwing stones anymore."

Belinda shook her head. "If they did, they'd miss the roof, they're that drunk. Or drugged. Students."

"Students?"

"I'm a teacher. Was a teacher. I'm retired now, it's too chaotic for me. I don't need students there" – she pointed to the wall her house shared with the other semi – "partying all night. Anybody wants this place they can have it. Errol

51

never wanted to sell, not after all the work we put into it. All we went through in the beginning. But Errol passed last year and I've had enough. We had thirty good years here. Time to move on."

It was none of her business, but she had to ask. "Where will you go?"

"You know, we put two sons through university. Time they paid their old mother back. I'm not worried about that. But who's going to pay good money for a house in this rundown neighbourhood? And let's face it, this neighbourhood is only going one way."

Charlotte sipped her coffee and ate a shortbread biscuit, then said: "What about renting it out?"

Belinda laughed. "Are you doing yourself out of a commission? No, I want to be shot of it. I can't see myself knocking on doors collecting rent."

"Then what about the people who own the other semi?"

"You can try. It's under sectional title so if he owns both he can consolidate. Makes it easy. Okay, try it. He's not the easiest to deal with. Once he put Satanists in there. We complained, he said 'What am I supposed to do about it?' And in the end, Errol got them out."

"How?"

She grinned at the memory. "Sent over some exorcists. Every day for a week. They scarpered after that, left owing a month's rent."

A day later she'd called on the other owner, a crusty old guy, retired, said he wasn't interested in buying but maybe somebody would take his semi off his hands, he'd had enough of that complaining woman who lived in the other half. So ... another client. She advertised the pair as a unit and she and Tony sold them a few weeks later to a developer planning to tear down both houses and build three floors of student digs, small studios with tiny balconies.

Laurence was impressed. She phoned him to ask what he thought she should do with the commissions she was earning. He mentioned fixed deposits. Or unit trusts. And lunch.

Lunch? She had to think about that. She'd only been on her own for six months.

"Just lunch," Laurence said, breaking the silence. "Nothing more."

"Of course," Charlotte said quickly. "I'd love to. Um ... the nanny won't stay on weekends unless I tell her in advance."

"We'll make it a weekday then," he said. "What about tomorrow?"

§

Laurence noticed at once how exhausted she looked, and said so.

"There's so much to do," she said defensively. "I don't want to be slapdash. I want to do this the right way, so I'm taking the course online at night, when the children are sleeping. Well, when Lianne is sleeping. Ian doesn't seem to need much down time. Anyway it's almost finished, and if I pass the exams, with my internship, I'll be certified. That's really important."

"And what will you do then? Go out on your own?"

"Not yet. It's too soon. Tony has a lot of information in the office that's really helpful, and costs a lot. I'd rather use what he's got. And I can learn a lot from him. Like how to identify who's likely to sell."

Laurence had settled on a New York sirloin. Charlotte was considering a salad, her usual standby, but Laurence said she needed something substantial, he could see she needed protein – "Do I?" she asked.

"Steak?" he suggested

"Oh no," she said. "I'm not up to steak."

"A small steak?" he said.

She shook her head. "Steak is for – I don't know – a normal life. A life of substance." She settled on a grilled chicken breast.

"Who's likely to sell?" Laurence asked when the waitress went off with their orders.

"Excuse me? Sell what?"

"You said there was a tool that shows who's likely to sell."

"Oh, right," she said. "Tony was very helpful in that regard. A couple living in a tiny house and they've just had their second baby and need more space. Well, that's not me. I'm not going to sell. Or an ancient couple who can just barely make it up the steps to the front door. That kind of thing."

"It sounds very creative," Laurence said.

Charlotte smiled. "I suppose it is. It's not designing a book or adverts for a milk substitute but I suppose you have to use whatever creativity you have left."

It was a worrying statement, but Laurence let it ride.

There was plenty of work for Charlotte. Selling houses involved more than putting pointer boards out on show days. Once she'd found buyers, she needed to check out their credit record before sending them to the bank for a bond.

And now that she knew what to look for, she could target people ready to sell, and hand them on to Tony who could help them find places to buy. As none of them had a great deal of money, he often handed them back to Charlotte, who listened to what they needed and tried to find likely places on the bottom of Tony's lists.

She found herself driving around suburbs just a small cut above the one where she worked, looking for houses for sale, noting who the agent was and phoning to ask whether she could send people there. She wasn't getting anything out of it, but years down the line, it would pay off.

"You're working too hard," Laurence said at lunch a month later.

"I have to," she said. "I don't want people to pity me and pity my children. And I want Charles to be proud of me. I want to show him that I can cope with everything – run his business and take care of the children. Keep it all together."

But she wasn't keeping it all together. She couldn't stand hearing Ian scream, so when she was at home, she carried on with demand feeding, generally in the middle of the night. In the end, she thought, it helped her to focus. Both children needed her, and by concentrating on what they needed, she was balancing her life well.

Until she wasn't.

She and Laurence had settled into a monthly lunch. One day he told her about a friend of his who did counselling.

"I don't need a counsellor," she said.

"Charlotte," Laurence said. "You've lost your husband. You've barely had time to grieve."

"Time to …"

"To miss him. To miss what it was like to live with someone you loved. To care for yourself. To –"

He stopped talking because Charlotte had begun to cry. Quietly. Tears rolling down her cheeks.

By the end of the lunch, Charlotte had taken the name of the counsellor. And although two hours once a week cut into the time she spent selling, she found herself looking forward to her sessions.

"You were right," she told Laurence. "There are so many empty spaces in my life, mostly emotional, I guess. I was so afraid of looking like a tragic figure I just forged ahead. I had to show people I could do it all, but I wasn't. Missing Charles, facing the loss of my husband – I wasn't doing that. Do you know, when I cried at our lunch two months ago, that was the first time I'd cried since Charles died?"

Laurence wasn't her only friend, of course; she began making time for her neighbours. Sharon and Bianca thought it great fun to help her stow the For Sale boards on Sunday evenings, then stay for supper. Meanwhile Charlotte got back in touch with her brother-in-law, David, and accepted invitations to Saturday lunches, bringing Lianne to see her cousins – one was nearly her age – and Ian, whom she'd finally weaned. Remarkably, he'd stopped screaming when he couldn't get what he wanted.

She'd also made friends with some of her clients, especially Mrs Smit, who was a joy. She'd moved in with her younger son, who lived in Sandton, and every so often they would go out for a meal. Unlike Laurence, Mrs Smit didn't mind if Charlotte only ate salads.

But Laurence had become her closest friend and one day he upped the ante, suggesting they go out for dinner and maybe a movie. "That sounds like a date," she said. "I don't think I can date."

"It's not a date," he said. "It's dinner and a movie."

"Oh. Okay then." She was fond of Laurence; she admired his financial acumen and was grateful for the advice he'd been giving her for more than a year. Basically, she owed him her success. Well, not all of it. Maybe the 30% Tony was now paying her, instead of the 18% when she'd started. But dating anybody would feel like betraying Charles.

There it stayed, for another six months. And then, when Ian, turned two, something changed.

She was now making a decent, if not excessive, income. She had no problem paying her bond and her children were happy, well fed, well looked after. Tony – aware that she was becoming well known in the industry – was talking about a 60–40 partnership, in an attempt to see off the big companies poised to poach her. She was now solidly in charge of her life.

And so she let down her guard and allowed herself romantic feelings. She didn't need Laurence's advice anymore; she could stand on her own two feet. That made her an equal, not a sad, confused widow in need of advice.

But she still needed Laurence – his warmth, his insights on all sorts of issues, his very solid bulk, the result of too many steak dinners. The world made more sense when he was around.

So she married him. And on a Saturday two years and a month after that terrible night when Charles collapsed, Laurence and his Jack Russell terrier moved into her house.

"I can't believe you've kept that dog in your flat all this time," she said, as it bounded off to find Lianne.

"Not so long," he said. "Just six months. What's a family without a dog? Uh-oh," he said, as his cellphone began buzzing. "Got to take this."

She shook her head, smiled, and went to the kitchen to grill the steaks.

5

Bogey and me

Jason and Simon

It was a mistake anyone could have made. Locking the car, Jason pressed the button on the wrong remote and shut the garage door. That would not have been a problem if he'd been outside, but he wasn't, and in his confusion, he panicked and dropped the remote.

He scrambled around on the concrete floor but it was too dark to find anything, and then he banged his head on the bottom of the back bumper. It didn't draw blood, nor did it damage the bumper, but the collision didn't help his rising terror.

Simon had been waiting patiently for their evening ritual, which began with sundowners and ended with supper, and when Jason didn't show up he went looking for him, fortunately arriving before Jason's meltdown was complete.

"I don't know what happened," Jason said, once he'd calmed down.

"Don't worry. It's over. Come have a drink."

Back when they were both working, they'd split up the more pleasant tasks that support life. Simon did the shopping. Jason did the cooking, unless he had a show on. Neither did the cleaning; that was Mumsie's job, and it kept her extended family of twelve alive.

But although Mumsie and Simon were still employed, Jason had thrown in the towel. He hadn't intended to stop working but he'd had a small stroke. Drawing on his training as an actor he repaired his speech in record time, but his movements were no longer as fluid as they had been. Actually, he limped. And, aside from *Richard III*, there aren't a lot of roles for an actor with a limp.

It was Jason's acting career that had brought them together. Simon was an actuary. He didn't find that as dull as it sounded to everyone he knew, but he did need to liven up his off-time – and theatre was a particular love. He'd seen Jason in a play at the Market Theatre about disaffected soldiers and thought him very good. He'd seen him at the Civic Theatre, as it was called then, in a Tom Stoppard play about journalism and ethics.

And then he encountered Jason at the launch of a novel by a mutual friend. Perhaps encountered isn't the right word – as soon as the speeches were over, he made a beeline for Jason, who had been browsing at the bookstore's magazine stand.

"You don't know me," he said, wrenching Jason's attention away from *Style* magazine. "But I've followed your career. If you're in a play I make a point of seeing it. You are simply superb."

The magazine went back to the rack. "I hope you're a critic. Or a talent scout from London, looking for new faces."

"Just an actuary who loves the theatre," Simon said. "Especially," now that he was standing a few centimetres away, "if you're in the play."

Jason smiled, a big, glorious smile. "I think this is the beginning of a beautiful friendship," he said, sounding very like Bogart.

And it was. Over dinner they discussed possible alternative endings for *Casablanca*, how it could have played out if it had been set somewhere less romantic – "Kempton Park? It's so convenient to the airport," Jason said. "Or Boksburg, a short taxi ride away? And Sam's café – what about the

Troyeville Hotel? The things that go on there, in Portuguese ... a good parallel. Or so I'm told."

"Why, what goes on there?" Simon asked, but Jason switched the topic to whether it would have been better if Ingrid Bergman's role had been taken by a man. "I would have been a brilliant Ilse." With the merest trace of a Swedish accent, he added, "With the whole world crumbling, we pick this time to fall in love ... Kiss me, as though it were the last time."

Simon didn't know what to say – "All right" was his gut reaction, or "That sounds like a good idea", but he wasn't used to being so forward. So instead, he said "It was the film of a lifetime."

Jason sighed. "We'll always have Paris. Or in this case, Joubert Park. And to me, you are Capitan Louis Renault, finding out who you really are. What you really want. And what you're ready to fight for."

"Malva pudding, I think," Simon said. "Although I don't think it's worth fighting for. But another bottle of this shiraz ... maybe."

Jason didn't let the allusion ride – basically, he never let anything ride. Throughout their 40-year relationship, when things began to slide – as they do, when people are together for a long time – when habit became a threat to what had brought them together in the first place, Jason would begin playing roles from plays and films they had both seen and liked. The best was Jason as the *Phantom of the Opera*.

And when that didn't clear the atmosphere he'd throw out more lines from *Casablanca*, changed to suit the situation – Peter Lorre as Ugarte, flogging visas to people desperate to get away: "You despise me, don't you?" or Bogey again "If that plane leaves the ground and you're not on it, you'll regret it. Maybe not today. But soon and for the rest of your life", or Bergman's "Kiss me as though it were the last time", flashing back to the way it had been in the beginning. It worked.

In fact most of what Jason did worked. His *King Lear* at Maynardville's Shakespeare in the Park one year set the standard for actors who came later and tried, unsuccessfully, to beat it. Simon had watched Jason turn himself into the addled old monarch, day after day, enveloping himself in the part, and took leave to follow him to Cape Town to watch the performance.

But Jason was not only an actor. He wrote plays that drew crowds to the small theatres he rented, directing and performing wonderful one-man shows or two-handers. For money, and sometimes for fun, he did voice-overs. He came back one evening claiming he'd done a voice-over for an underground porn film, and had loved it. "It was five different men," he said, "so I had to do heavy breathing five different ways. Four, actually. For the fifth, I was running out of breath, so I moaned. Repeatedly."

He was inventive, coming up constantly with stories about his fellow actors and directors, or former lovers, or politicians he'd gone to school with. The stories were always outrageous and some of them may actually have been true.

"That minister," he'd say, as still another talking head showed up on the SABC, justifying homelands. "I saw him in the toilets at the City Hall last week. With a rent boy. And not just any rent boy. This one is prodigious, he works all the time, can take on two johns at once. You should have heard the minister. Screaming 'Again! Again!'"

"What were you doing in the toilets at the City Hall?"

"Having a piss. What do you think I was doing?"

Simon's analytical mind kept finding holes in Jason's stories. Like the one about a director he'd had a run-in with – "He had a fight with his wife at a party, and later they were speeding along the M1 and he pushed her out of the car. She's in hospital on a ventilator. Not sure she'll live."

"How did he open the passenger door if he was driving?"

"He's got arms like an ape," Jason said. "You've never seen arms like that on a human being."

Then there was the war criminal his grandmother had spotted shopping at John Orr's. "He was a leading member of the Ossewa Brandwag. Ouma remembered him."

"Whatever we may think of them, the men in the Ossewa Brandwag weren't war criminals, not technically." Simon said.

"But the Nazis were. Didn't I say that? He was with a Nazi war criminal, shopping for perfume. And you know all the perfumes of Arabia ..."

Simon couldn't believe his luck, that he'd wound up with this exciting, vibrant man. Okay, sometimes it was a bit much, and when he felt exhausted by Jason's three-ring circus he'd stay late at the office of the reinsurance company that so valued his talents that management kept promoting him. He would immerse himself in probabilities – to his mind solid, grounded largely in statistics, in mathematics and logic.

But that happened rarely. What made Jason such a good actor, besides his excellent memory, was his intuition. He could see when he was going too far, and then he'd haul out the braai, the steaks and the beers – even in the dead of winter.

And often he'd invite his sister Renee, because for Simon, she was family.

Simon had no family to speak of – or to speak with. When his parents died in a road accident soon after his twelfth birthday he didn't feel particularly abandoned, since they had never shown much interest in him. He'd been a boarder from the age of nine, first at Cordwallis, then at Michaelhouse. His parents had left plenty of money in a trust to continue keeping him there and to pay for university.

His aunts and uncles didn't know what to talk to him about, not even at his parents' funeral, and his cousins had their own lives. Lawyers, not relatives, ran the trust.

Simon didn't miss what he'd never had – until he met Renee.

Renee clearly adored Jason, and Simon became part of the package. Her children called Jason Uncle J and Simon was immediately Uncle Si.

It was a delight watching her trade barbs with Jason, or play Maria to his Tony, singing duets with him. Renee sang beautifully but had bowed to her parents' view that one actor in the family was enough. Now she had a family of her own and could do as she liked.

And Renee was in awe of Simon. As an accountant, she knew very well the work that actuaries performed. Predicting future events accurately so that companies knew what to do with their money required not only a superior grasp of mathematics but also a wide-ranging knowledge of almost everything, from politics to psychology to the possibility of storms in the Pacific. And actuaries worked with statistics, which had been her least favourite subject at university.

Renee's husband Glenn was a quiet GP with a dry sense of humour who enjoyed trading arcane, technical stories with Simon. Their son Alex was as rowdy as his uncle J and their daughter Pamela, two years younger than her six-year-old brother, took to following Simon around like a puppy.

Simon was initially puzzled, then embarrassed, but soon just grateful as he was absorbed into Renee's family. They didn't come to Friday night dinners every week – sometimes Jason had a show on, or there was a party, or they just felt like staying in. But the door was always open – and when Pamela, who had followed her uncle into the theatre, bought a house nearby, there was the occasional Sunday brunch.

§

They were at dinner at Renee's two months after the incident in the garage when Jason suddenly left the table and walked out the front door. There was a stunned minute of silence before Simon went after him.

"Was it something I said?" he asked, finding Jason on the pavement, heading for home.

Jason looked at him blankly for a moment and then said "OMG, what am I doing out here?"

"Not a clue," Simon said. "Come on, let's finish our dinner. Renee said she slaved for hours over the curry."

"She's lying, of course. You know she bought it in. Fortunately."

A few days later, Glenn asked Simon to stop by his surgery alone, and when he did, Glenn went straight to the point.

"Has Jason had any more episodes?"

"Of walking away at inappropriate times? Not that I recall," Simon said, and then remembered Jason's confusion in the garage. "But that may have been the blow on the head – he hit his head on the car."

"And what else?" Glenn asked – because he could see there was something a bit wrong. "Before that. A change in his behaviour."

"Actors aren't like the rest of us," Simon said. "It's hard to know if they're serious."

"So there has been a change."

It felt like a betrayal, talking about it, but Simon had been concerned for weeks. "Jason needs to know where I am. All the time. I assume it's because he's bored, not working."

He was silent for a few moments. Glenn waited.

Then: "He repeats stories – he's never done that before. And in the kitchen the other day he stood staring at the cinnamon and asked where the cinnamon was. He was very upset when I told him he was holding it in his hand. He should have laughed it off. I think he's worried."

"So am I. Can you get him in to see me? I'm not a geriatrician but I can do some initial tests."

§

To Simon's surprise, Jason said tests were a good idea. "What if it's the stroke?" he said. "Maybe it's concussion. Maybe it's dementia."

"It's not dementia," Simon said.

"Let's find out," Jason said. And when the initial tests Glenn performed were not conclusive, Jason agreed to see a geriatrician, as long as it was Shereen, a GP who lived a few streets away and was studying part-time for a diploma in the speciality. "Look, I'm over 65. Let's see what her tests are like. Can I walk a straight line? No," he said, and did a weaving waltz around the braai. "Can I count backwards from 90 by sevens? Of course not. Why would I? Why would anybody want to count backwards?"

Part of the test was to draw a clock, and that part he passed, but barely – his minute and hour hands were the same length, and he left out 5, which he insisted was the most boring part of the day and also much too early to be awake.

In any case, Shereen told Simon, whom Jason had insisted be part of the consultation, that it looked like early stages of dementia.

"Alzheimer's?" Simon asked.

"Maybe. Alzheimer's is a form of dementia. There are other sub-categories. There are even sub-categories of Alzheimer's. It's too early to tell. But Jason will need to be monitored."

"I'll tell him," Simon said.

She looked at Simon for a full minute, then shook her

head. "No. Send him in. It has to come from me."

Jason was inside for a good half-hour, and when he emerged, he was quiet, and thoughtful.

"Should we talk about it?" Simon asked, as they headed, together, for his car.

"Give me a moment," Jason said.

The moment stretched to a month. And then one day Simon realised he and Jason were researching the same websites.

"It's duplication," he said. "What's the point of duplicating our research? Jason, we have to talk about this."

"All right. I'll research Lewy Body Dementia and you can learn about Creutzfeldt-Jakob."

"That's not what I meant."

Jason gave him the sort of look he had reserved, in the past, for directors who tried to tell him what to do.

"You're right," Simon said quickly. "There's nothing to talk about. Let's split up the research."

After his stroke, Jason had spent weeks writing on an A4 pad. Simon found it one day when Jason was otherwise occupied, strolling round the block, back into his earlier love of walking. The notebook was full of the same few paragraphs, written over and over. Early entries were unreadable, but later entries were better, and eventually his writing was clear.

This time, it was his memory Jason was working on. He was spending hours in the garden, reciting – sometimes declaiming – passages from Shakespeare: *Othello* ('Behold! I have a weapon ...'), *Coriolanus* ('You common cry of curs! whose breath I hate/As reek o' the rotten fens, whose loves I prize'), the Prologue from *Henry VIII* ('I come no more to make you laugh: things now/That bear a weighty and a serious brow/Sad, high and working, full of state and woe ...'). That one made Simon worry.

"Shereen's pills are working. And he's getting better," Simon said, as he and Glenn stood in the garden after dinner so that Glenn could smoke his cigar in peace.

"Don't get your hopes up," Glenn said.

"He's reciting long passages from Shakespeare. I think if I asked him he could still do *King Lear*, all of it. All the parts."

"Let's check on the bougainvillea," Glenn said. "I don't know why we bother. We've never had any success with bougainvilleas."

They walked to the bottom of the garden. The bush was bare of bracts, although there were plenty of leaves. Glenn shook his head, turned away.

"Simon, Jason is not going to get better. He will get worse. Prepare yourself."

§

Jason was in a state of great excitement one night two months later when he shook Simon awake. "It's an eclipse!" he shouted. "Why weren't we told?"

Simon, groggy, could only groan. Finally, "What time is it?"

"Who cares? This is a momentous moment. Darkness at noon."

Simon grabbed his watch. "Jason, it's the middle of the night."

"It's midday, and it's dark! It's an eclipse! Look!" He pulled back the curtains. "See? Where's the sun?"

"On the other side of the world," Simon said. "Australia. Here in Parkview, it's the middle of the night."

Jason opened the window, breathed in the cold air, smiled, and turned back to Simon. "This is where we don't agree," he said.

It was the beginning of the decline. One day he couldn't find his phone, which was in his pocket. He wasn't sure how to use it anymore.

"Who do you want to call?" Simon asked him.

"Whom," Jason said, and dropped the subject.

Then he forgot what the toilet was for, and spewed the walls of the bathroom with urine, like a child discovering how much fun it could be. Simon cleaned the bathroom, then cleaned Jason.

"You need to get a caregiver," Renee said. "You need to get out sometimes."

"I've often wondered what the point was of having inherited a fair whack of money, and made even more," Simon said. "Now I know. I will never have to work again. I can look after Jason."

"Not all the time. I can call the Alzheimer's society, they have people who can look after him for a few hours. It gives you a break."

"I don't want a break." Simon tried to explain. "Jason was ..." He stopped, then started again. "Jason is my life. I think I can say that with some authority. We shared a life for nearly 40 years and I cherish him. It's a privilege to care for him now that he needs me."

Shereen advised Simon to enter Jason's world. If he saw things that didn't exist, for example, Simon should also see them.

Simon tried. When Jason said he was convinced there were bats in the attic – although they had no attic – Simon said yes, he'd phoned the bat society to come and get them out.

Jason glared at him. "Don't humour me," he said.

The end came soon afterwards. Jason had been Bogey in *Casablanca* again. "It doesn't take much to see that the problems of two little people don't amount to a hill of beans in this crazy world," he'd said. "A hill of beans. I've often wondered what a hill of beans would look like."

Simon was on his way to the bath, and when he emerged half an hour later he found Jason gone. He was frantic. He typed out a plea on the Parkview WhatsApp Group, then joined a search party to look for him.

Maybe Jason had intended to visit the Zoo, or perhaps he was looking for a hill of beans, but he didn't make it across Jan Smuts Avenue.

"That must have been really rough on the taxi driver," Renee said, after the funeral.

"Mom, that sounds callous," Pamela said, and hugged Simon.

"What do you think you'll do now?" she asked later, as they walked in her parents' garden.

"I don't know," he said. "We married for practical reasons – we both assumed I'd go first. So there isn't much I have to do about the estate. Jason wanted you and Alex to be cared for, and I'll make sure of that."

"We're fine, Uncle Si," she said. "Don't worry about us. We worry about you."

Simon closed up the house, closing out the memories, and travelled in Europe – Amsterdam, Berlin, Prague, Paris, finally London. Six months later, opening the door to the house he and Jason had shared, he reached back for his suitcase and realised he'd left the airport without it.

There had been forebodings during the last few months with Jason but he'd shoved them to the back of his mind. Jason needed him. This was not the time to panic.

Now the issues were front and centre – his problem remembering where he'd parked the car – not once, but often. The terrible smell in the kitchen which he'd tracked down to the oven, where a chicken he'd bought had gone not into the refrigerator when he unpacked the groceries but into the oven where it had sat, still in its wrapping, for a week. The day he couldn't remember his ID number, or the pin number on his credit card.

When he mentioned it to Glenn the first Friday night dinner after his return, Glenn told him that Renee had noticed. "We're prepared for it," Glenn said. "The cottage awaits."

"I wouldn't dream of imposing," Simon said. "Anyway I have a house, you know."

"And when you can't cope anymore? Simon, it's going to happen, you know that. We can send a caregiver to look after you at your house, but we'd be happier if you'd move into the cottage. A big bedroom, a lounge, a kitchen ...

"I'll be fine," Simon said.

He went home, put the car in the garage and pressed the button on the wrong remote, shutting the garage door instead of locking the car. He pressed it again, the door opened and he went into the house, poured a glass of shiraz and thought about Glenn's offer.

Perhaps his issues were the result of stress. He'd managed Europe well enough, although he did lose his hotels and AirBnBs often – but he was a tourist in strange cities, so getting lost could be expected.

Suppose what had happened to Jason was happening to him? Suppose he'd kept the symptoms of dementia at bay while Jason needed him, and then when Jason was beyond help there was nothing stopping him from giving in to whatever was happening to his brain. He was of an age and as an actuary, he knew the probabilities – he'd worked out the statistics when Jason's struggles began.

He knew the trajectory of his illness, if indeed that's what it was, could be quite different from Jason's. There was an easy way to tell: he'd phone Shereen in the morning.

"You're our brother-in-law," Glenn had said earlier, offering the cottage. "You're family. We can't let anything happen to you."

Jason had bequeathed Simon a family.

"I wouldn't put it that way," Glenn said, and Simon realised he must have been thinking out loud.

"It's a bit late in the day to impose ..." he began.

"There's no imposition involved," Glenn said. "You've been a member of the family since the first time Jason brought you to dinner. Should we carpet the lounge in the cottage, or are you happy with quarry tiles? Renee wanted me to ask you. Come, let's have a drink and talk about it."

Okay, Simon thought, back in his house. They're not going to change their minds. That's how it is with families, I guess. Not too late to learn.

We'll see how it goes.

6

Soaring lessons

Amy

Amy married her boss. He was 25 years her senior but a vibrant, handsome, exciting man, far more interesting than guys her own age.

They had met in Lesotho, where Greg had gone to gamble and Amy, a Benoni blonde with a B.Ed degree from Wits, had gone to teach. When he returned to Johannesburg Greg convinced Amy, via a mix of Skype calls and emails, that devising training programmes for his financial services firm would be more fulfilling than her current job, which consisted of filling in at a private primary school whenever a teacher was ill or on vacation or burnt out.

Six months after she started at Greg's company, they were married.

Amy doted on Greg – on his experience, his knowledge of art and politics, on his get-up-and-go manner, on the new worlds he introduced her to. They went often to the theatre, which was so much more satisfying than television or films. They saw plays in Sandton, in Newtown. They went to experimental works at the Wits Theatre in Braamfontein.

Greg was not a boerewors-and-pap or burgers-overcooked-on-the-braai man. Consequently, Amy experienced some truly excellent wine and fine dining.

And she learned quite a lot about art, which would come in handy one day when she needed money to survive on.

For there are two major downsides to marrying an older guy. One is the baggage – one or more ex-wives and children who think you're after his money.

Greg had two ex-wives, two sons from the first wife and a daughter from the second. The sons, close to Amy's age, hated her, while the daughter – at 16, very unsure of herself – secretly contacted her for advice on the sort of issues she assumed Amy would be an expert on: makeup, clothes, what to say when a fellow student phoned "just to talk" or what to do when he sent Instagram shots of his body clad only in a very tight Speedo as he was about to plunge into the school pool.

The second downside is the older husband's rate of deterioration, which does not match yours. It is likely you will be widowed while still relatively young – and so Amy was.

Greg had a heart attack while sitting on the couch drinking an after-dinner coffee. Amy had the presence of mind to call the paramedics but although they came instantly it was no use.

The bank froze Greg's account when the bank manager spotted his death in the obituary columns. Amy was outraged. "What am I supposed to live on?" she asked the bank manager.

"You have enough money in your account," he said, and handed her a prayer card. "Just pray to Jesus for help in this terrible time. The Lord will provide what you need."

She was fortunate that Greg had had the presence of mind to insure the house, so that the bank – and not Amy – was responsible for paying off the bond. Also there was life insurance, but it might take a while to be paid out. Meanwhile, she had been named as co-executor – with the lawyer – of the estate, and he would be arranging a letter from the Master of the Court to that effect. It wouldn't help with money or shares or any other intangibles of Greg's wealth, but if she wanted to sell, for example, Greg's car, the letter would make clear that she was entitled to.

That's when she began an inventory of what she could

sell. The art – much of it could go on auction, although she would hold on to the pieces Greg especially valued. What about Greg's car? Surely a two-year-old Porsche 911 Turbo S Cabriolet would fetch enough to keep body and soul together?

She photographed some paintings and sent them off to an auction house. An assessor made an appointment to view them in situ, took away the two Irma Sterns, the Peter van der Westhuizen, three William Kentridge drawings and the Mark Rothko, as well as a Henry Moore sculpture, and promised her she would never have to work again.

Amy wasn't so sure. She sold Greg's Porsche.

Now she could relax, and grieve, and think about what to do with the rest of her life.

But not yet. The day after the car was sold, Greg's daughter Melissa phoned, sobbing. Her mother hated her, she was ugly, she would never have a boyfriend, and she was failing natural science.

Melissa's mother had gone to Paris for a week – Greg had been very generous to his ex-wives – and so Amy drove over in her Toyota Yaris, picked Melissa up and took her shopping for clothes, followed by lunch and a bracing talk.

"Just look at your lovely hair," she told her. "I wish I had such beautiful hair. It streams, like silk. Look at your hands – those fingers, people would pay to have such delicate fingers. And your eyes – hazel is the best colour of all."

It seemed to work. "Sixteen is terrible," she told her. "Seventeen will be better. And eighteen will be the best. Let's find you a new lipstick and a natural science tutor."

That task accomplished, Amy went to bed. For a week.

"This is ridiculous," she told herself midway through Day Seven. "Get up. Get dressed. Go to the greengrocer at least. And maybe the supermarket. Somewhere."

On Day Eight, that's what she did. And perhaps, should

not have done. For somewhere near the lettuces she ran into the wife of a couple who had often invited her and Greg to dinner parties, and while the woman said "Oh we must get together again," it was clear she didn't mean it.

In the juice aisle there was a woman she'd played tennis with. Again, there was that fake "We must get together sometime". Amy smiled, agreed, and turned in time to see a man she used to know duck behind the frozen vegetables.

What were they afraid of, Amy wondered. When we went to someone's house, I always directed conversation to the wife. Was it the fear that I was now fancy free? As if ... and she began to cry, and stopped that line of thought.

Money was not a problem. Although Greg's will included generous bequests for everyone – both ex-wives and all three children – Amy would receive the lion's share. Melissa phoned to tell her that Greg's sons, Freddy and Charles, both in their twenties and gainfully employed, had talked about contesting the will, once the lawyer informed them what they would be getting, but that the lawyer had said they hadn't a case.

"How do you know?" Amy asked.

"Oh, I was there," she said. "We all went to the lawyer's. Mom and me and the boys. I think they really resent not having it all."

§

The next day, Amy tried to work up the courage to reach out to some of the people she and Greg had spent a lot of time with. No one had phoned since the funeral. She had embraced Greg's circle when she married him and now it looked as if none of his friends was ever going to phone. She'd give it one more try. What did she have to lose?

She phoned a woman whose husband Greg had played tennis with every week, inviting her and her husband to dinner. They were busy that weekend, and the next, and then were probably going away for a while. She phoned someone who had come to the funeral and cried buckets, hugged her, said "We must get together, you poor child". She and her husband were off to Europe for a month and would phone on their return.

After the third rebuff, she knew. People had just been tolerating her. That life was over.

What would Greg have done? He would have taken the bull by the horns ... she had a sudden vision of Greg wrestling a bull to the ground, and had to laugh, and then couldn't stop laughing.

"Okay," she said to the living room. "I'm no longer the third wife of a wealthy executive. I shall have to reinvent myself."

How?

"I'm tired of feeling sorry for myself. I'm going to think positively," she told the remaining Kentridge, a desolate landscape done in charcoal and red pen. "Whatever comes, I will say Yes to it."

Something would present itself. Inspiration, or the Universe, would take care of things.

Or maybe she shouldn't wait for the Universe to get around to her situation.

She made a quick inventory of her interests. She didn't like games, was not particularly mad about food, basically found fashion boring. She'd gone to a gym once and hated it. But during the year in Lesotho, she'd taken to hiking in the Maluti mountains – even in winter, when the peaks were snow-covered. And she'd loved it. She'd loved the scenery, the exercise – but mostly the challenge.

The next day she found a hiking club online. The name made her smile – Friends of Doris – so she phoned and asked if she could come along on their next outing. It would be in the Magaliesberg.

She had four days to buy hiking shoes and a metal water bottle – time enough, but she almost didn't make it, because the next day Melissa showed up on her doorstep, sitting on a small suitcase.

"I hate my mother and she hates me," Melissa said. "Can I come live with you?"

This was not what Amy had considered when she'd decided to say yes to everything, but there it was, so she swung into action – the mode that had made her such a valuable employee.

First she phoned Gwen, who said she was welcome to Melissa, who was the most irritating teenager in her experience. "She'll eat you out of house and home," Gwen said, "but I'm sure you don't need any help from me, considering how much Greg left you."

Amy didn't throw the phone at the wall, but instead phoned the hiking club, who said a 16-year-old was okay, just old enough to manage.

Melissa said she didn't want to go. "You have a choice," Amy said. "You can hike with me, or you can go back to your mother. I'm not leaving you here on your own. That's not the way this works."

It meant a considerable outlay on an extra pair of hiking boots, but properly outfitted, they showed up at the starting point. There were about a dozen people, mostly guys and all in their thirties, like Amy, and they welcomed both Amy and Melissa with enthusiasm.

Melissa discovered she quite liked climbing up and down koppies with a bunch of guys. At one point Amy had to show her how to pee behind a bush but all in all it was a brilliant success. Jerry took special care of Melissa, helping her up difficult bits, showing her how to slide down on her bum without damaging her coccyx, and pointing out, just in time, a puff adder sunning itself on a rock in the middle of the path.

The school run didn't go quite as smoothly. Amy had to be up at dawn to drive Melissa 10km to school and be back in the car at teatime to fetch her.

But climbing took care of Melissa's lack of confidence – and it absorbed much of Amy's depression.

It was liberating. And so were the people – a mix of civil servants, academics, activists and foreign students – not a CEO among them. The conversation ran along the lines of how long it would take hiking boots drenched in the river to dry, when the group could stop under a tree for a water break, what people had brought for lunch, and which Sasol garage they should stop at for ice cream on the way back. Now and then the conversation would veer into music or politics but nothing lasted very long – there were koppies to climb, wonderful scenery to take in, trees to shelter under.

In weeks, the hikes escalated – from koppies to hills, and then a couple of people suggested a trip to the Drakensberg, overnighting in a tent.

"You're going to have to go home," Amy said. "Just for the weekend. I can't be responsible for you on something that strenuous. Especially as you're new to this. You're not ready for crampons and ice axes ..."

"Ice axes?" Melissa said. "And what's a crampon?" Reluctantly she returned to her equally reluctant mother, and Amy went off with seven other hikers, including Jerry and Mel and Sue.

The hike was a bit more daunting than the earlier ones – they climbed up a sheer cliff at one point on an iron chain ladder. (Could have used pitons instead, Amy said to herself, and smiled. She'd been researching climbing techniques.)

She remembered how to put up a tent, and the small pup tent she and Sue occupied went up before the guys had theirs in place. She knew how to braai, but let the men do it.

Sitting around the regulation campfire, getting grease on her shirt from the ribs and the chicken bits, Amy thought she had never been happier. All those years with Greg, her idea of roughing it had been an air-conditioned tent with ablutions en suite at a luxury game reserve in KwaZulu-Natal. And here she was, filthy, her hair going at odd angles, her clothes a mess …

"Everest," Jerry said.

"Not quite," said Sue. "One cliff, darling. One ladder. Big deal."

"No, I mean Everest, as in Everest," Jerry said. "I've always wanted to trek to Base Camp."

"You do that," Sue said. "Mel? Should he?"

"As long as he doesn't expect me to go with him," Mel said.

"I could go on my own," Jerry said. "But it's better to share it. What about you, Amy? Are you game?"

"Oh, absolutely," Amy said, caught up in the moment. It was, after all, never going to happen.

Until it did.

It took a year and a half, but Jerry made all the arrangements, found a guide and applied for the permits, on the assumption that Amy had meant it when she'd agreed, and one afternoon, as two dozen Friends of Doris spread out opposite a waterfall in the Magaliesberg to eat their sandwiches, he asked Amy if the fee was too high for her. It wasn't.

"There's a lot of climbing through snow and ice," he said. "Can you handle a fortnight of snow and ice?"

It was a bit late to ask, but she shrugged it off. "It won't be a problem," she said. "Layers. I'll just wear layers. Stuffed with down."

That left one issue.

"Jerry, honestly, do you think Mel will mind?"

"I think it's more likely he'll be relieved," he said. "Mel was afraid I'd ask Jeremy. Or Howard. He's not worried about you."

"Nobody's worried about me," she said, smiled, and took another bite of her tuna on rye. "Even I'm not worried about me."

Melissa had gone to UCT to study business economics – clearly her father's daughter. With time on her hands, Amy had been looking for something useful to do, but the education department wasn't interested in finding a place for someone who might be here today and gone by April.

So when the date for their departure arrived, Amy was more than ready. She'd worry about the future after they'd descended from Base Camp and flown home. Because there was no doubt in her mind that they'd make it up to Base Camp. She had no desire to try to climb to the summit. Those people who did were probably mad. But Base Camp – that was good. And exciting enough.

§

Kathmandu was complete chaos – cars, bikes, rickshaws, driving at great speed on both sides of the dusty potholed road, weaving in and out among people and donkeys.

They were first in line for the flight to Lukla the next day – altitude close to 3 000 metres – to start their trek. "I believe this is the world's most dangerous airport," Jerry said casually, as the twin engine plane stopped short of the mountains looming, it appeared, just a few metres away.

"Nice to know, now that we're on the ground," Amy said. She was trying to keep her excitement under wraps.

Of course Jerry had arranged for a guide. Dipak met them at the airport and led them on a three-hour hike to a tea house in the next village, where the main dining room was warmed by a furnace fed with yak dung. He showed them their room – a plywood box with a double bed and a single blanket.

"Uh oh," Jerry said.

"It's okay," Amy said, "we can cling to the edges."

But they didn't. At Jerry's suggestion, they lay nose-to-toe. Snuggling, sleeping bag to sleeping bag, got them through the night. It was a pattern they repeated at every stop, as the rooms grew colder and colder.

The next day, they hiked up to Namche Bazaar, at 3 400 metres. Amy began to flag and Jerry offered to carry her backpack but she demurred, dragging it up the stone steps to the tea house.

When they set out again after two days of acclimatisation, they found swing bridges before every village, long flights of stone steps and the occasional narrow ridge, shared with yaks laden with goods. Dipak told them to stop and give way to the yaks, who had been known to push hikers off the path – and it was a long way down. Amy used those encounters as a chance to stop and catch her breath.

The tea houses were pretty much identical – plywood walls, furnaces in the dining rooms, ablution facilities down the hall or outside. There was no hot water. Jerry had had the foresight to bring plenty of baby wipes, which were okay for a couple of days but not for the entire trek.

"It's surprising what you can get used to," she told Jerry, after braving a freezing cold shower.

Six days after leaving Namche Bazaar they hiked through a snowstorm and down slippery stone steps to a tea house in the village of Gorakshep, at just over 5 000 metres, where they would be staying while their bodies got used to the thin air. Only then would they be considered fit enough for the final push to Base Camp, which they had been able to see from the trail – the brightly coloured tents and flags and the famous Khumbu icefall in the distance.

The next day dawned with blue skies, or so Jerry told Amy, who lay in bed for a while, listening to the bells on the yaks delivering supplies to the guest houses.

The days of acclimatisation were the best for Amy. She wandered the streets, catching her breath, buying fruit and Snickers bars and trying to engage local people in conversation. She was picking up a bit of Nepalese – hello, how much, would you like a Snickers bar? And wherever they stopped, she also picked up a trail of small children who, indeed, would like a piece of chocolate.

"I think I'm in love," she said to Jerry, on the morning they set out for the final push to Base Camp.

Jerry looked alarmed.

"No, silly, not with you," she said. "Mel's safe. No, it's Nepal. I think I'm in love with Nepal."

"It's too cold for you," he said. "I keep worrying you're going to turn into a block of ice."

"I'm okay with it," she lied. "It was cold in Lesotho too, you know. Well, in the winter."

They set out in a state of great excitement, despite the snow that began to fall when they were nearly there. But Base Camp turned out to be a big disappointment. Serious climbers preparing for summit attempts were not very welcoming to wimpish trekkers, who were treated like day-trippers – which, in fact, they were.

"I don't suppose they'll offer us a cup of coffee?" Amy said.

"Come on," Jerry said. "Let's go back."

Tracing their path back to Kathmandu, but more quickly this time, with no need to acclimatise – they passed struggling trekkers on their way up to Base Camp. On one long and steep section through the national park, Amy wanted to assure them it would get easier, but the trekkers kept to themselves, concentrating on saving their breath and keeping their feet from slipping.

Amy didn't, and suddenly felt a shooting pain in her left foot. There was nothing she could do about it with a couple of hours of hiking left, so she carried on in agony. At last they arrived at the guest house. Sitting near the furnace in the dining hall, she could finally take off her boot. She'd only twisted the foot, not the ankle, she was relieved to see, but it really hurt, and she rubbed her foot vigorously to take the pain away.

Two tiny children who had been racing around with sticks, pretending they were horses – or maybe donkeys – noticed Amy, stopped playing, came over and stroked her ankle. They looked ineffably sad. "It's okay," Amy said, moved by their concern, hugged them each in turn and handed over a Snickers bar.

In the days that followed, on the trail and in the guest house in Lukla, she couldn't get the children out of her mind. In Kathmandu and Lukla, in the bigger towns, one could see even small children sharing iPads and teenagers with an ear glued to a mobile phone. But in the hill villages, sticks had to stand in for even the most basic toys. What happened when they reached school age? Were there even textbooks, much less iPads? Was there a future for these children?

"There are schools," Dipak told her, when she asked about facilities in the hill villages. "But they struggle. The government wants the children to be taught in English, because it is the language of the future. But the teachers don't know English well enough to teach in it."

"What about mother tongue?" Amy asked him.

"We have a lot of mother tongues," he said. "Twenty or thirty. Look, I'm fortunate. I live in Kathmandu. My second brother is at MIT in America, studying civil engineering. When he starts making money, it is my turn."

"Are you also going to MIT?" she asked.

"I haven't decided where to go," he said. "But I'll leave engineering to Krishna. I am more interested in hospitality."

Jerry weighed in. "I'm not sure where this conversation is going," he said, "but the shuttle's about to leave."

Five hours later they were in Kathmandu, and a few days later, back in Johannesburg.

It was easy for Amy to adjust to Johannesburg's altitude, after climbing above 5 000 metres, but everything else seemed out of joint. What was she supposed to do with the rest of her life, without Greg?

One day, she started to email the provincial education department, then scrapped that idea. She wanted to teach, not spend the day in the staff room, which is where the teachers spent most of their time when she did her practical training in Soweto. She was in the classroom because she was a student teacher, but the people who were supposed to supervise her were nowhere to be found.

Meanwhile Jerry and Mel were getting married – Mel realised that he could have lost Jerry under an avalanche or down a crevasse.

"Will you be my Best, oh, I don't know, Person?" Jerry asked Amy.

"I'd be honoured," she said. "Do I have to arrange a stag night?"

Jerry laughed – and then she could hear him over the phone, shouting her question to Mel, and she could hear Mel laughing too. "I think we can skip that," Jerry said.

"Flowers then," she said.

"Just bring wine," he said. "Next Sunday. At the house."

The impending wedding concentrated her mind. What did she really want out of life?

The next morning she phoned Dipak, who was home in Kathmandu after taking some clients from Japan on a four-day trek. A couple of days later he phoned her back. That's when she bought a one-way ticket to Kathmandu, promised the lawyer she would stay in touch, and phoned Charlotte, the estate agent who lived on the next street, to offer a sole mandate. She'd met Charlotte at the odd dinner party, back when Greg was alive.

"You're mad, you know," Charlotte said, walking into the house minutes later. "I don't want to lose a sale, but there's plenty for you here."

"Like what?" Amy said. "People who hide from me at the supermarket? Greg's daughter doesn't need me anymore. Anyway, she's in Cape Town. Which reminds me – if she'll do all the paperwork, she can have my car. I'll leave the keys with you and I'll give her your contact details."

"But Nepal," Charlotte said. "They're not the only ones who need good teachers."

"Please don't tell me about how much good I could do teaching in Soweto. I've been that route. Wait, I think the coffee's ready."

They took it out on the stoep, watching doves chasing smaller birds away from the bird feeder.

"When I graduated, I could have applied at any of a number of private schools," Amy said. "But I wanted to make a difference, and I wanted adventure, so I went to Lesotho. Did you know I spent a year teaching in Lesotho? Nepal is like Lesotho. Or anyway it could be like Lesotho. Just – Charlotte, if you can sell the house, please sell it. Otherwise just rent it out."

"This will be easy to sell," Charlotte said. "Everybody wants to live in Parkview."

"Not me," Amy said. "Not anymore."

They drank in silence. The winter sun was shining directly onto the stoep. Just beyond was a garden well stocked with winter flowers blooming under stately old trees. There was not a cloud in the sky. "Amy. I don't know you that well. But how can you leave all this?"

"Nepal is a mess, physically," Amy said. "The infrastructure is crumbling. The streets are even more potholed than ours, the pavements are filthier than ours – even in Kathmandu, rubbish isn't picked up on any kind of schedule. But you know what? There's not the cynicism we live with here. Or if there is, I missed it. I don't know why, but the country really grabbed me and held on tight."

"Do you know what you'll be doing there?"

"I might work something out. In the hill villages maybe I can make a difference. Dipak is trying to get me some kind of post. He has an uncle in the education ministry who is always complaining that nobody wants to teach in the villages."

The day after the wedding, she was gone. A month later Melissa took possession of the car, and six months later there was a new family living in the house, a young couple, Charles and Emma, with four-year-old twin sons.

One day Emma came across a delicate loosely woven shawl in blue, purple and pink, and called the estate agent. "It seems to come from Nepal," she said. "There's also a very nice Buddha. Shouldn't we send them on?"

"No worries," said Charlotte. "She probably left them for you."

"What about the prayer flags? There's a string of them folded up in a drawer in the kitchen. I think the boys would love them."

"My advice is to put them up," Charlotte said. "Maybe they work. You never know."

"I don't know," Emma said. "I think I should save them for her. Just in case."

"Not a problem," Charlotte said. "There's plenty of storage space. But my bet is she's not coming back."

7

Endgame

Muriel

It was on a Wednesday afternoon in August that Muriel made up her mind. There was still a bit of sunlight, but shadows were beginning to slant across the veranda when she took her rooibos tea out to a cane table and straight-backed chair, gazed at the garden and ran through ways to kill herself.

The tea lasted longer than the list. She could only think of the obvious: hanging, shooting, sleeping pills. None would do. She didn't own a gun, had never taken sleeping pills, and as for hanging ... no. Unpleasant. Mind you, there was a time when that was the only way out. Her contemporaries ... but they were all gone. That was the issue. She was the only one left. She'd lived too long.

All gone, even the pets. There was that elderly librarian, although not as old as she looked, with her white hair cut short and severe. What was her name again? Gypsy, the dog was Gypsy. Funny, one remembered the name of the dog but not the librarian. Gypsy collapsed and died one Friday morning. A week later the librarian was gone as well. Just like that. How did they do it, these old folk? Dodgy hearts, probably. Just her luck – a strong heart, good lungs, nothing likely to kill her. Unless she did it herself.

Someone was rattling the street door, ten metres away. She watched for a moment, then went inside. All very well, these reveries, but one had to eat.

Or maybe not. A Martian opening Muriel's refrigerator

would assume a household of first-year university students. There were several cheeses in various stages of decay, loosely wrapped in waxed paper. Small stained plastic containers held unidentifiable substances, some with chunks, some without. Vegetables had been shoved into corners to rot quietly out of the way. Only the eggs, meat and milk showed evidence of care: the eggs in a plastic egg-holder, ham and left-over chicken wrapped in foil, a half-full milk carton in the refrigerator door.

When gorillas began soiling the nests they made anew every night, it was evidence of a declining population. Muriel had read that somewhere – George Schaller, perhaps, or Dian Fossey. She would have to look that up. Later. Personally, she had attributed it – even when reading it – to despair. When old ladies no longer look after their refrigerators, it was time to shuffle off.

But first she'd boil a couple of eggs, sauté a slice of ham … that would do. And tomorrow she'd begin her research. Life was a gift, she knew that; but it was a gift she felt obliged to return.

Several hours later, she was moving books aside in the massive yellowwood bookcase in the living room. What had she done with her copy of *Gorillas in the Mist*? And it was autographed, surely a valuable item to lose. Poor Dian Fossey; she stopped in Johannesburg, gave a stunning lecture, autographed copies of her book, then went back to Rwanda where she was murdered not long after. A year or two, at most.

Gorillas and their nests … it was more likely in George Schaller. Where was *The Year of the Gorilla*? Why couldn't she find anything anymore? It was hopeless – the books had been placed, over the years, wherever she could find a convenient space. She'd have to switch on the computer. Tomorrow. When her head was straight.

She flicked the switch that would turn on the alarm and the electric wire along the top of the wall. Did it matter anymore? Perhaps. It might be time to die, but she did not want to be caught unawares.

The next day there were errands to run – telephone bill, rates bill, the electricity account to pay. She'd never been able to bear owing anyone anything, even now, when it wasn't going to matter very much.

She disliked going to the post office, but it became clear there was no alternative when she'd mailed a month's worth of cheques and they'd never arrived. Well, they'd arrived somewhere; quite a lot of money had disappeared from her account.

She dropped the bills and the cheques in the box set out for paying bills, exited and headed for her 15-year-old BMW. A young man was leaning on it, chatting up a young woman sitting on the bonnet. It must be awfully hot, Muriel thought, but all she said was "Sorry?"

The woman looked startled. "Ma?" she asked.

"Sorry, but it's my car," Muriel said, "and I'd like to leave."

"O-kaay," said the woman, with enthusiasm, and hopped off, helped by her suitor, who whispered something in her ear. They both looked at Muriel, and laughed.

At the first traffic light, there were only five hawkers and two fellows giving out handbills. No beggars. Not too bad. The light changed before they reached her car.

The second traffic light turned yellow as she approached and she was tempted to carry on through, but a lifetime of training is hard to wipe out in an instant, and she stopped.

The young man selling a string bag of avocados got to her first. She'd bought them once, out of pity, and they had never ripened. No point buying them out of season. Anyway, the last thing she needed was food.

"Sorry," she said, "I don't need any avocados."

"Only R50," he said, "for you, Ma. Special price."

That irritated her. "I'll say it's a special price. They're usually R30."

"I'm asking you to support me. You drive a nice car. I haven't sold a pocket all day."

"I'm not surprised, at that price." Suddenly she felt exhausted. "Sorry, no. Try someone else."

Before the light changed, she was approached by a man selling children's puzzles, another selling strawberries, a young white man – surprise! – with a placard reading "My cat's in jail for stealing my neighbour's chickens, and I need bail money", and a street child trying to look pitiful. She made sure her window was shut after the strawberry seller, but it made no difference – people would come right up and stare through the glass.

As the light was changing, the street child tried to smash her window, but he'd waited too long. She could see there was something in his hand, probably a spark plug, but it glanced off the window as she moved away.

She was more cautious at the stop street a block from her house and looked around before bringing the car to a brief stop. She'd had her wooden garage door electrified decades ago before she became too feeble to lift it; and her late husband had pulled out all the bushes growing in the vicinity so they would have a clear view of robbers lurking behind the shrubbery, waiting to slip under the door. The street was empty.

Once in the garage, she sat behind the wheel for a good 20 minutes, wondering how one would feed in carbon monoxide. Dorothy Parker had never come up with that method, she thought – only razors and rivers and drugs – "razors pain you, rivers are damp, acids stain you", etc. Perhaps she had thought of it, actually, but "carbon monoxide" didn't scan.

The next day Muriel hauled the garden hose into the garage and tried to match its fittings to the BMW's exhaust pipe. One end was far too big, with the nozzle that fitted a tap; and the other end was too small. The hose itself was stiff, after a couple of decades lying out in the sun. It was difficult to manage, placing the small end as far as possible into the exhaust pipe, and moving the nozzle end into the front passenger window. She'd get it just so far, and the small end would slip out of the pipe. "How do people do these things?" she said aloud, and then she thought of a hand towel, to keep it in place. That worked; and a bath towel took care of the gap at the top of the window.

Using monogrammed towels was not the advice offered by the suicide site she found on the internet several hours later. In fact the site recommended venting a space at a point farthest away from the source – whatever that meant. She read on: it would take anywhere from 30 minutes to three hours. For heaven's sake, what does one do for three hours, sitting in a car and waiting to die? Read a book? And what if one dies before the denouement?

The site was very enthusiastic about suicide by carbon monoxide, because then one could die anywhere – including "a favourite scenic lookout". Imagine.

Only one problem: catalytic converters. If her car had been fitted with a catalytic converter, it would take even longer for the carbon monoxide to build to a fatal level. Had it? How could she find out? It was all getting very complicated.

There was a poison that had been getting a great deal of play in the newspapers some time ago, something called "two-step". Apparently it worked so quickly that you could take only two steps before it killed you. Where one would get it was not clear, although Muriel recalled a story where a young reporter had bought a packet from a street hawker.

Perhaps down on Diagonal Street, or the eastern end of Market and Commissioner, where the muti shops were. It was worth a try.

She remembered the way to the city centre, of course. Years ago, before the white flight to shopping centres in the suburbs, she had been one of those women the newspapers always wrote so dismissively about, who wore a hat and gloves when meeting other ladies for tea at John Orr's.

She found a space behind a line of taxis. It was an inspired location: where there were taxis there would certainly be hawkers, and sure enough, one could hardly walk on the pavement for the crush of them. One fellow, whose face was buried in a copy of the *Daily Sun* (headline: Rats ate my baby), had quite a lot of unlabelled packets. She homed in on him.

"Tell me," she said, and he looked up, startled. "Tell me," she began again. "Have you any of that poison called 'two-step'?"

He shook his head, waved her away.

"Well then, who would have it? Do any of these hawkers around here carry 'two-step'?"

"It's illegal, Ma," said a voice behind her. She turned; the man who had spoken towered over her. He looked like one of the taxi drivers; she could picture him at the wheel, an elbow casually draped on the door, talking to somebody in the passenger seat as he weaved in and out of traffic. Or perhaps he was a queue marshal. "What do you want it for?" he asked.

"Rats," she said. "There is a rat invasion at present." This was true. There was often a rat invasion.

"Take my advice," said the man. "Go to the Pick n Pay and buy rat poison. Stop making trouble here."

He took her arm and steered her back to her car. "Get back in your car, quickly now. See those makwerekwere?"

She looked where he was looking: a knot of young men staring at them. "They want your car, and your handbag, and your jewellery. They don't care if they kill you. We don't want trouble here. This is a peaceful taxi rank. Give me your car keys."

"Surely not," she said, as the man unlocked the car and manhandled her inside.

He shook his head. "Just go," he said, and handed her the keys. "Go."

But that was the point, she thought, pulling into her garage. Dying, that was the point. Why was it all becoming so difficult?

The next morning there were flower beds to weed – she would go out in style. But once down on her knees, she realised she was going about it the wrong way. "Weeds flourish because they're strong and healthy and have taken root in a suitable environment," she said aloud, to nobody. Why had she never thought of it before? Weeds belonged where they had taken root. It was the delicate flowers she had been protecting all her life from weed encroachment that ought to be removed.

She started back to the house. Someone knocked on the street door. She hesitated, halfway, then continued across the lawn. She'd have to wash up a bit before going along to the petrol station to ask whether her BMW had a catalytic converter.

Did the attendants know what a catalytic converter was? Probably, but it wasn't knowledge they were willing to share with her. She asked to see a supervisor, and he admitted having heard of a catalytic converter. It was his opinion that her car was of a vintage that might have predated the installation of the devices. "Ah," she said. "That's all right then. One doesn't want to spend too much time in the car, waiting." And she smiled.

Seeing the smile, and the relief, he said "I can't be sure. I wouldn't put my life on it."

And that's what she was intending to do, and very soon. Perhaps she'd bring a book with her after all, she thought, in case the man was wrong.

It wasn't far from the petrol station to her house, but it was far enough. She looked incuriously at the open bags of rubbish dumped under the trees, at the litter on the grass verge – the issues she used to bring to the attention of the city's department of health, not that it changed anything.

It was not quite a smile, perhaps more a lifting of one corner of her mouth. It was an acknowledgement that she would not have to see the litter ever again – not the used condoms, or the sweet wrappers, not the styrofoam boxes containing half-eaten hamburgers or chicken bones, not the cosmetics bottles or the used nappies.

Even on such a short route, there were taxis, and when one cut her off and then stopped, abruptly, the corner of her mouth raised again. Seeing she was trapped behind a taxi in a suburban road, a man came up to her car window, trying to sell her strawberries. She looked at him without registering, and at her blank look, he turned away.

She had just put the BMW away and gone into the kitchen when the phone rang. Funny, that – it never rang anymore. But she was courteous, so she answered. Someone trying to sell her something – was it insurance? Was it satellite television? The man on the other end spoke, and Muriel answered. But she could not have told you who he was or what he'd said. And by the time she made what she intended to be her last cup of rooibos, she'd forgotten all about it.

She was sitting on the straight-backed chair on the veranda, sipping bush tea and going through a checklist of where she'd put the hose and which towels to use, when someone knocked on the street door, and rattled the handle.

She stopped, the cup halfway to its saucer, and looked at the street door. "Will I still be doing this next week? And the week after? And next year?" she said aloud – choosing towels, finding a book, making sure the hose didn't slip out of the exhaust.

For the first – and last – time in her life, a short cut appealed. So she finished the tea, put down the cup, strode to the door and opened it.

Later that day her body was found just inside the street door by a neighbour who had been pushing a pamphlet through the letterbox when the door swung open. It had not been shut properly when the intruders hurried out with a few items – a flat-screen TV and her computer, not much else. Ironically, or perhaps not, the pamphlet was a notice for a meeting about a new security company called CAP which deployed armed men dressed in black who patrolled the streets in 4x4s, 24/7. The discovery of Muriel's body galvanised the generally laid-back neighbourhood into signing up.

As for the police, to no-one's surprise, they never caught her killers.

8

The reboot

Myrna

Riverends was not an especially elegant establishment – more like a subsidised housing estate, but a really good deal for someone who had spent her life as a legal secretary. Perhaps if Myrna had married one of the lawyers she worked for – or if she'd finished studying law instead of leaving university to marry the man she'd fallen in love with – she would have been able to afford something better. But she had never regretted her decision to marry Eric, an electrician with a gift for bringing everything from cars to computers back from the brink.

Eric adored Myrna – her braininess, her ability to cut through nonsense, her talent for success at whatever she took on, and close to the top, her cooking. Myrna found Eric a lot of fun and amazingly tolerant of her foibles, for example her tendency to fill their semi with stray creatures – dogs, cats, many lizards, once a few rabbits that had escaped from a hutch in a nearby school. One day, he thought, he'd find a lion in the lounge.

Most of their mates lived in upper-middle-class suburbs grouped together as The Parks – Parkview, Parkhurst, Parktown West and North – but these were way beyond their budget. They stayed in an eastern suburb that had gone from Italian to largely foreign Africans married to local women and carefully avoiding townships for fear of xenophobic outbreaks. The suburb was slowly deteriorating, but it was perfectly positioned for their son Holden because

King Edward, the best government school for boys in Johannesburg, was just across Louis Botha Avenue, and his karate dojo was only a ten-minute drive away.

The house had a grapevine – it was one of the reasons they'd bought it. Where there were Italians, there were Catawba grapes, which the Italians made into wine. She'd used the leaves to make dolmades, and once, to scoop a spider egg pouch off a window ledge so Holden could throw it into the empty stand across the road. Holden might be a devoted karateka but he would not stand for anything to be killed, not even spider eggs.

Myrna loved the neighbourhood, whether Italian or African. She joined a street committee, and when she was asked to do research on issues – bylaws, who owned which derelict building, that kind of thing – she managed to find the time.

She also found time for Eric's true passion, travelling up Africa in their ancient grey Land Cruiser. Big Grey had well over 200 000 km on the clock but it carried them to a dozen countries.

In the early days, they always took Holden along. He learned to love the continent – from the Kruger National Park to the lava fields at Lake Turkana in Kenya.

In time, Holden sailed through university, became an IT boffin and emigrated to Canada.

After he left, Myrna and Eric continued their African odysseys. The last trip took them into Ethiopia, with many adventures, some of them not so hot, like an oil leak – poor Big Grey, maybe time to retire it? – and a tyre that exploded into shreds on a corrugated road to Addis Ababa.

It was in Addis that Eric fell ill. It wasn't malaria. It wasn't TB. Nobody could figure out what it was. But it was time for Myrna to take charge. She sold Big Grey, bought airline tickets and got Eric back to Johannesburg. He died in an

ICU ward a week later.

Eric had said he didn't want to be 'planted', so a cremation was arranged. And Holden, who had flown in to keep his mother upright, insisted the ashes be scattered in a place his father loved. Tanzania and Kenya were too far to go with a mother still in a state of shock, so they drove up to the Botswana border and flung Eric's ashes into the Limpopo.

Holden offered to stay for a while, but Myrna said she could handle things like the hospital bills on her own, so he returned to his wife and job but phoned every day or two, checking on her.

Meanwhile she went over the bills carefully, querying items added after Eric had died, lab bills for processes not carried out and bills from one cardiologist who – as she saw, as she sat by Eric's bedside – looked at the chart and signed it without so much as glancing at the patient to see if, perhaps, he was still alive.

The animals helped. By the time Eric died, there were only two cats, but they did what they could, shredding bills, rubbing against her ankles, sitting on the computer keyboard. They were stretched out on her desk when the retirement village she'd contacted years before on a whim phoned to say they had a place for her.

She hadn't planned on leaving the neighbourhood but it seemed a sensible move. The house held too many memories. She hadn't realised until returning from the Limpopo how much her life had revolved around Eric, how he had always been there for her, looked after her – without him, who was there?

They had shared so much in their lives together, including a joint almost every night: smoking on her own was depressing. Every morning, waking in the bed they'd shared, she expected to find Eric up and on his way to the kitchen. If she wasn't careful, she'd expect him in every room, round every corner. This way madness lay.

Time to reboot.

So she went to Riverends, liked the small cottage that had just become vacant, signed the offer to purchase and transferred the deposit. The lawyers she'd worked for had arranged a pension, and she had long been putting money into a retirement annuity, so she'd be okay – not well off, but okay.

"You're leaving," said her friend Charlotte, an estate agent, dropping in one morning for coffee.

"I think so," she said. "Sorry, but I'm not getting any younger. I'm on the wrong side of 70. I suppose I'm old."

"You don't seem old. Well, maybe, since Eric passed on, but you'll bounce back. We all have to. Myrna. Have you noticed people have been turning single family homes in this area into rooming houses? This isn't my territory" – answering Myrna's question before she could ask it – "but I can make an arrangement with a guy I know who sells in this area. In fact on this very road. Let me get you a good price for your house."

And that was it. Two months later, Myrna paid the final amount for her Riverends cottage from the money the buyer paid for her house and began directing the renovations.

Could she have a wood floor? No, said the carpet-and-flooring fellow Riverends had recommended. He offered plastic laminate with wood-grain veneer, and at a prohibitive price. "Take it or leave it," he said. She left it.

What about the kitchen cupboards – too high, too low and too deep, with tons of wasted space. Could those be changed?

"With pleasure," said the kitchen contractor. And then didn't do it.

Eric would have made sure it happened or he would have done it himself. Without Eric … it was a train of thought she had to nip in the bud. This was a new life, a complete reboot. Embrace it.

And she tried. There was no grapevine, but the cottage came with a large sun-washed stoep where she could hang her beautiful orchids, and a lovely garden where she could plant the roses she loved – red, white, peach.

In her garden at home, the roses had surrounded the dagga she nurtured as a cost-saving measure, but she thought Riverends would not be impressed if she'd planted a crop here. In any case, smoking without Eric ... she'd have to find a new vice.

Meanwhile, there were benefits. The cottage had huge windows on the world and a bedroom large enough for two wheelchairs – this was, after all, a place for people on the edge of falling apart.

There were friendly guards at the gate with a talent for remembering names and unit numbers.

There were birds in the trees, weavers making nests and tearing them down, plovers clicking, mossies hopping, robins calling.

But there were no animals.

"When I signed up," she said to Daphne, the interface between management and the residents, "I was told I could bring my cats."

Daphne wasn't interested. "You've paid already," she said. "If you want your money back you'll have to see the accountant. You won't get all of it back."

"I was told I could bring my cats. You can't just change the rules like that. Not after I've paid."

Daphne sighed. "We did a survey last month because some people were complaining. So we banned pets. We have feral cats to keep the mice away. Don't feed them. And water birds. Walk around. You'll see. People are happy here."

Myrna panicked. For years she had been the go-to person

for unwanted beasts. She had adopted Cinnamon after one of her Saturday mornings volunteering at the SPCA. He had been terrified, crouching in his pen; she'd lured him out of hiding and then couldn't give him up.

The other cat, Charcoal, had been brought by a team of young guys who often played soccer in the street. "He's been following us for two days," said the striker. "We don't know how to take care of animals. But you do, Mama. Here." The vet said it was a Russian Blue.

She'd met Charlotte's friend Bianca a few times at Charlotte's house, and once she'd come to Myrna's. She showed up again fortuitously the day after Myrna's discussion with Daphne.

"We went onto the website last night and it said no animals," Bianca said. "I love your cats. Please can I have them? You can come and visit them whenever you like. We have a dog but he likes cats. I think. No, I'm sure he'll like your cats. Who wouldn't like your cats? Sharon's going to love them."

It was the last problem to be solved, and at the beginning of spring, Myrna moved into her Riverends cottage.

"There's such good security. I'm so happy to be here," said Phyllis, dropping in one afternoon with a cake. "Aren't you happy to be here?"

People tended to drop in uninvited, but as Myrna didn't know anyone, it wasn't such a bad idea. Nobody seemed particularly interested in finding out anything about her. That was okay. She'd always been a good listener.

Phyllis's name had been moved up the list after a robbery. Charmaine's husband was in the early stages of dementia, so she could talk to Myrna but only at her cottage, where he could see that Charmaine was around – and only for a short time. "Aren't you happy to be here?" she asked, not expecting an answer.

Wanda's son had insisted on employing a live-in caregiver. He was very talented and very successful, owned three restaurants that were doing fabulously well, and his sons were at Michaelhouse because he was really too busy to look after them and her daughter-in-law was, well, we won't talk about her.

Maryanne had been at Riverends for two decades. A robin hopped into Myrna's lounge as she and Maryanne were having coffee one afternoon. Maryanne leapt up shouting "Get out! Get out!" and the bird took flight.

"They come into my lounge and make such a mess!" she said crossly.

"Why don't you keep the door closed?" Myrna asked, a bit surprised at Maryanne's reaction. She was happy to see birds hopping around on her tiles.

"Why should I? So, I was telling you about my son. He's a cardiologist in LA. He has so many famous clients. Movie stars, you know? Like ..." and couldn't remember the names.

Myrna went back to the subject of birds. At least, she said, they were around, unlike cats and dogs. At least there was some nature at Riverends.

"Oh there used to be cats here. And dogs. I complained for years," Maryanne said. "They make such a mess."

"Cats don't make a mess," Myrna said.

"And what happens when the owner dies? Who's going to look after them? Not me, I'll tell you that for nothing."

Maryanne played bridge. So, on a rough estimate, did 80% of the residents. When the welcoming committee called on Myrna, their first question was whether she played bridge.

"I don't," she said, "but I'd love to learn. I do play chess. Is there a chess club?"

There wasn't a chess club, nor were there bridge lessons. She would have to find them elsewhere, and join the bridge club once she was up to speed.

"We have a lot of activities," said the welcoming committee leader. "I'm sure you'll find something to suit you. Everyone is so happy to be here." She handed Myrna a few sheets of paper and the committee departed.

Myrna read through them. A gardening group that put plants in pots. A painting group. Bingo. Trips to drama at Montecasino – and if you didn't like what was on the stage, Sibyl told her, you could nip out at the interval and play the slot machines. Twice a week a bus took residents to a local shopping centre, and if they were quick about it, they could shop and stop for coffee before being herded back onboard.

There were pub quizzes – that sounded interesting, even if there was no pub – and a chair exercise group, sometimes films and – oh there it was, religious services. Visiting priests and rabbis but, she noticed, no visiting imams.

Myrna had stocked up on seedlings and equipment, planning to grow the odd salad. It seemed a nice day, so when the welcoming committee left, she decided to begin: and found the canvas bag that had held her small spade, rake and secateurs gone. The tools were neatly piled next to the potting soil.

At least they've left the seedlings, she thought, and set to planting spinach, tomatoes, parsley and basil.

A quick wash, and then a walk to the mailbox she'd been assigned, where she became engrossed in notices on a pinboard. It had adverts for everything from comfortable shoes to hearing aids. There were offers of wheelchairs and scooters for sale, and requests for garages for people who needed somewhere to stow their oxygen equipment.

Where am I? she asked herself, briefly. Hearing aids? Comfortable shoes? She took a deep breath – no need for oxygen equipment, not yet – and opened her mailbox for the weekly schedule of events.

And there she found Quiz Night.

§

When Myrna paid her money at the door she was sent to a table that had a gap. Each table held six people, and this one had only three, two women and a man, the husband of one of the women. At the very last moment, a woman using a walking frame slid in next to Myrna. They named their group a silly suggestion from one of the women – The Jolly Punters – and then proceeded to win every round.

The woman with the walking frame, it turned out, was a whiz. Brenda, her name was, and between Brenda and Myrna, there was very little they didn't know, from the year Elvis Presley died to the capital of Slovenia. More, Brenda was brilliant at deciphering anagrams and Myrna could easily see which number belonged where in a sequence, and how they'd been jumbled up. They were both good at identifying faces of 1960s film stars.

The morning after Quiz Night, Myrna was grinding coffee when Brenda arrived.

"I never touch coffee," Brenda said, but when it was ready, she said she'd give it a try.

Myrna poured a cup and watched as Brenda took a tentative sip, then added milk.

"I see you have a sewing machine," she said.

"I make most of my clothes," Myrna said. "I used to make my son's shirts when he was too small to object."

"There's a sewing circle here, you know," Brenda said.

"I didn't know," Myrna said.

"They seem to specialise in children's clothing. And toys. They're actually quite good. They meet sometimes in the library. That's next to the coffee shop. Have you tried what they call coffee in the coffee shop?"

"Where's the coffee shop?"

"I see you haven't been on the other side of the lake. It's next to the restaurant, which is next to the frail care centre. Which I hope I never need."

"Maybe I should try it," Myrna said.

"Don't. The food is just passable and I believe the coffee is undrinkable. Unlike yours. This is actually very good. I gave up coffee years ago but I might take it up again. No, I never go down there. It's too much, seeing them sitting there in their wheelchairs all day. It's not for me. And something tells me it's not for you either."

"Well, maybe not," Myrna said, although she was intrigued. "Have you been here long?"

"Too long. Time to move on."

"Are you leaving? I didn't think anybody ever left a retirement village."

"I might. It's too easy here to sink into lethargy. No one to take care of. No husband, no child. No pet. Everything is taken care of for you. So you begin taking pleasure in small things. And in routine. On Tuesday launder the sheets, on Thursday – before dawn, mind you – water the garden. On Wednesday, mince for supper. On Sunday, chicken. I had enough of routine in the convent."

"Was that St Theresa's in Rosebank? I suppose there was no Sacred Heart back when we were in school."

"Not a convent school," Brenda said. "A convent. Ten years, two breakdowns. I wasn't meant for The Life, so I left."

The next day Myrna went looking for the library, and as luck would have it, found the sewing circle there. She joined on the spot. Mostly they were making toys – giraffes were much in demand, as were wild dogs and train engines. Myrna was thinking of slipcovers; Sibyl's daughter, it turned out, ran a fabric shop so whatever Myrna needed could be supplied at cost.

Afterwards she walked down to the coffee shop, where

there were many people sitting around, not all of them in wheelchairs. She spotted a couple who had been at her table for Quiz Night, Mike and Christi, and they invited her to join them for lunch.

"Don't you love it here?" Christi said. "We love it here, don't we, Mike?"

"We do," Mike said. "There's everything you need here. I was hesitant at first because you have to wait until someone dies to get a place. They call it the turnover."

"That's quite an image," Myrna said, and smiled.

"It's a horrible thought," Christi said.

"But then I realised it's the wheel of life," he said. "Somebody will get our cottage one day when we die."

"Oh, don't talk about it," Christi said. "What about a prego roll. Should we order prego rolls? What would you like, Myrna?"

Christi and Mike were both retired primary school teachers, and they both coached grade twos at a school nearby – Christi in reading, Mike in mathematics. "The classes are too big now, you see," Mike said. "The teachers can't cope. And I wanted to give something back. We've had a good life."

He smiled at Christi, who beamed back.

Myrna tried not to tear up – she missed Eric every day of her life. But sentiment was not her strong point.

"I do like it here," she said. "I only wish I could have brought my cats."

"We all miss our pets," Mike said. "I fought against the ban. I thought because I was chairman of the residents' association people would listen."

"There's a core of old ladies here who can't be bothered with anything and they carried the day," Christi added. "And Lenka supported them, of course."

"Now she's doing her best, Christi," Mike said firmly.

"It's hard to run a place this big on such a tight budget."

Myrna filed away the news that Mike ran the residents' association, and asked who Lenka was.

"Lenka's the general manager," Christi said, and wrinkled up her nose. "She makes life as easy as possible for herself. Of course she wouldn't allow animals, even if the vote had gone the other way."

"The feral cats have territories, I've noticed," Myrna said. "My section is patrolled by a very big marmalade cat."

"Some of the residents feed them," Christi said, "although we're not supposed to."

"Sounds like a good idea," Myrna said, filing that information away as well.

It was the last time for a while that they would sit at the same table, or indeed, eat out. A week later, Johannesburg went into lockdown, and so did Riverends. The coronavirus was out there somewhere.

The viruses were winning outside, but not at Riverends. Residents were not allowed out into the larger, more dangerous world, and no visitors were allowed in. Deliveries were left at the gate, as were visitors, who talked to their parents and grandparents through the bars of the fence bordering the road.

Myrna noticed a lot of empty flats and cottages as she walked in the grounds to keep from going nuts. Presumably many of the residents, seeing the lockdown coming, had fled to their children. Unfair on the kids, perhaps, but much better for the old folks to have that human contact.

The supermarkets kept sending her emails, offering to deliver. "Should I?" she asked Bianca, who phoned her every few days. "And how are the cats?"

"Taking over," Bianca said. "The dog's afraid of them. Look, there's no choice if you're not allowed out."

"Expensive, isn't it?"

"Isn't everywhere?"

Unpacking her first delivery of provisions, Myrna thought she could get used to the luxury, but perhaps without the schlep of sanitising all the packaging, and then herself. She had no desire to catch the virus, not at her age, so she followed Bianca's recommendations to the letter. It took her half an hour to make her groceries safe the first time. Afterwards, she got better and faster at it.

She had always been afraid of dying, something she'd kept quietly inside while going along on Eric's death-defying trips. She was grateful and surprised she'd got this far, and she was punctilious in taking precautions: if the rule was two metres, she would honour it. She ordered in a mask and gloves online for the moment when Riverends would let its residents go out to the shops.

She had bought a pile of novels the day they were warned that the lockdown would be coming; and it was good to delve into a fictional world where there were other challenges, but not a virus, or anyway, not this one.

The news on television was terrifying – the virus knocking off huge swathes of the population worldwide, including children. What must small children think of a world, she wondered, where a human touch could kill them, where they had to suit up, mask up, to go outside?

It gave her an idea. She emailed the members of the sewing circle to suggest they try to make masks as interesting as their beautiful toys: a bunny mask with ears, perhaps, or a duck mask with a beak.

The first picture appeared on her cellphone a week later – Sibyl had done a pink pussy cat, complete with whiskers. Then came the front view of a train engine from Lucille, and a duck mask with a little orange beak from Susan.

One month into the lockdown Myrna made an appointment to see Lenka – a new regulation. Masked and gloved, she walked through Riverends' deserted grounds, arrived at the appointed time and showed her the photos, holding her phone so that Lenka would not risk catching the virus, assuming she had it.

"Very nice," Lenka said.

"Will you please put something in the newsletter so the residents can buy them for their grandchildren?"

"The newsletter is not a shopping guide," Lenka said.

"The price is minimal. And it keeps the women busy."

"Absolutely not," Lenka said. "If I do it for them, everyone will want to advertise in my newsletter."

Myrna scanned a couple of photographs, printed out copies of the photos and a note about who was making the masks and where residents could buy them, and stuffed a copy in every mailbox. Two days later every mask had been sold and the sewing circle was busy making more.

Meanwhile whoever was lifting bits and pieces from her stoep seemed as free to move around as she was. In the weeks under lockdown she'd lost a pair of gardening gloves, the rake and three tomato plants. The thieves didn't seem interested in the parsley. That was a win.

At last, the lockdown slipped down to a reasonable level and seemed on its way out – it would remain, in some form, for another year, but the regulations were now bearable. Masks would be required for the foreseeable future and Myrna decided the sewing circle's children's masks deserved a wider audience. A mention in the local knock-and-drop newspaper would no doubt elicit many orders – and among other things, it would be good publicity for Riverends.

She mentioned it to Christi and Mike at their first post-lockdown coffee.

"We'll probably need to check that with Lenka," Mike said, so Myrna made her way across the grounds to the manager's office.

The policy instituted during the lockdown was still in force: one had to make an appointment to see the manager. Fine. Myrna made an appointment for the first available time, which Daphne said would be in an hour, because "She's very busy. You can't just walk in, like she's there waiting for you."

When Myrna returned, an hour later, Lenka had gone out. "It was an emergency," Daphne said. There was no telling how long she would be.

The emergency appeared to be a nail appointment, because when Lenka walked in an hour later, she was reluctant to handle the pages Myrna offered her, although her nail varnish was almost certainly dry.

"What is this?" she asked.

"The sewing circle's children's masks are flying off the shelves. Everyone here seems to have grandchildren."

Lenka smiled. "Nice," she said.

"We're thinking of trying for a wider distribution, maybe an article in the local newspaper," Myrna said. "It would be good publicity for Riverends. If people know about the high quality of work produced here …"

The smile disappeared. "Oh no," Lenka said. "You can't do that."

"Why not?"

"It would put so much stress on the residents. Oh no. We don't want any problems on that score. They're here to relax. We're happy if they find hobbies, of course. Something they enjoy that isn't too … stressful."

"There was no stress," Myrna said, getting irritated now. "They actually enjoyed it. It got them through the lockdown."

"The lockdown is on its way out, dear," Lenka said. "And I have another appointment in" she looked at her watch "20 minutes."

"So it's all right if they make wonderful masks for children but they mustn't make too many?"

"These are elderly people. Their working days are over. They're here to take it easy."

Myrna was fuming when she knocked on Brenda's door. "That woman," she said. "I bet her next appointment was with her hairdresser. You could see her roots growing out."

"Why do you think I'm leaving?" Brenda said. "We're supposed to putter around, just stay out of the way, and wait for God to collect us. Lenka thinks this is God's waiting room. If the highlight of your day is going to bed, turning off the light and drifting into sleep, there's something very wrong here. Death will be very easy for these people."

She was in full swing. "I don't know about the men, but women need something to nurture, or what's the point of staying alive? Did you know that people die years sooner if they don't have a pet? They've done studies. Proved it. I can't understand why someone like you is here. Why aren't you leaving too?"

"I've thought about it but honestly, I'm too poor. For what my cottage cost me here, I'd probably get a very small two-room flat with no sun and no garden. Nowhere to plant my roses."

"That's something I've been meaning to mention," Brenda said. "Have you been missing things?"

"I have, actually. How did you know?"

"It's the Adamses. Have you encountered them? Perhaps late at night, digging up your plants? I call them the sticky beaks. They're absolutely shameless."

"Somebody made off with my tomato plants," Myrna said. "Not all of them. They left two."

"They were probably hoping you wouldn't notice. When the woman who lives opposite went into frail care they were there that very night, digging up her roses. They've stolen from most of us in this section. I think they do it for the fun of getting away with it."

A week later, following Brenda's directions, Myrna walked past the Adams garden, a good ten minutes away, and there, among a jumble of gnomes, rose bushes, gazanias, mismatched plastic chairs and two braais, she spotted six large pots, one holding three tomato plants – and her canvas bag.

She thought briefly about marching up and taking back the bag, at least. But it seemed a lot of trouble for something so minor. Already, she was keeping her gardening gear inside.

And so far the "sticky beaks" had left her orchids alone. Let them just try to pinch the orchids – then they'd know the meaning of justified wrath. She'd learned a lot from the street committee.

She went to tell Brenda what she'd seen but the cottage was empty. "She's gone," said a passing cleaner, Rita.

"She said she was leaving," Myrna replied, puzzled that Brenda hadn't said goodbye.

"One day here, next day in hospital. Next day gone," Rita said. "You think the coronavirus is over but it's not over."

"But she'd had her vaccinations ..." Myrna said, suddenly unable to take it in.

Rita gave her a look, and went on her way.

It took several hours for Myrna to process Brenda's death and to face the reality of living in a complex designed for elderly people. The turnover, as Mike had put it, would be constant. Could she stand it? Was the reboot working, or should she just abandon the effort and see what she could find with the money from the sale of her cottage?

§

Bianca phoned two days later, inviting Myrna to visit her cats now that Riverends was allowing her out.

It was good to be in the world again, driving down

Jan Smuts, turning in at Zoo Lake, passing the Alliance Francaise. She parked next to Art Africa and was heading for the bottle store on the corner when she stopped outside a shop selling pink ballet tutus for little girls, taking in the hustle and bustle of the street – young people shopping, stopping to talk, teenagers in school uniform, laughing.

As she stood there, another woman stopped and asked: "For your granddaughter?"

"No granddaughter," Myrna said, turning around. The woman was holding onto a small boy, who was mightily pulling. "Isn't it great to be outside again?"

"May the schools stay open," the woman said fervently, and let herself be pulled away.

Myrna smiled and walked back, stopping to buy roses for Bianca at the vegetable shop and at Art Africa, a wall clock painted with a curled crocodile.

She'd opened the boot to put her purchases away when she remembered.

Holden was not much older than the little boy she'd just encountered when he swam with crocodiles at Lake Turkana.

Not intentionally – they'd been warned that there were crocodiles in the lake, but young Kenyan kids were in the water so it was probably safe.

Then the pelicans and goats that had been basking on the shore disappeared.

Eric spotted a crocodile heading their way – okay, smaller than Holden, but a croc all the same. Myrna had barely had time to panic when Eric had hauled the kid out at a speed approaching Big Grey's fastest.

Holden tried to pull away from Eric – he wanted to go back into the croc-infested water. The Kenyan kids laughed. The crocs, they said, never bothered anybody.

It was ... a memory. It was then. This, perhaps, is now.

She put the clock and roses in the boot and drove on to the house Bianca shared with Sharon.

"So how is it there?" Bianca asked. She'd put the roses in the sink and was setting out strawberry tarts and a pot of Earl Grey tea.

"It's better than I thought it would be," Myrna said. "Not much in the way of enrichment and entertainment, though."

"Do they let you grow your own dagga?"

"It didn't seem like a good idea," Myrna said, and smiled. "I don't think those people would know what it was, but what if somebody there recognised it? They'd probably throw me out."

"Good," Bianca said. "Then you could buy a flat here. Oh, here come your cats. If you moved back into the world, you could take them back."

The cats looked healthy and happy; they glanced at Myrna and then walked away.

"I don't think they're my cats anymore," Myrna said.

"They're very independent," Bianca said.

"You're making excuses for them."

"Probably. So what about moving to Parkview?"

"I don't think I can afford it. But … I can visit."

"Often," Bianca said. "Do they let you out at night?"

On the way back, she wondered what life would have been like in Parkview, rather than in the neighbourhood where she and Eric had raised their son. It would have been nicer, perhaps easier, in this child-friendly suburb, but that would have required a different husband and a different life, and she was content with the one she'd had.

She didn't actually belong in the world outside, not at this stage of her life. Even the cats had sensed it. It was good for a visit, and she'd do that often. But it was time to commit to the reboot, and to life at Riverends.

Back at Riverends, Myrna missed Brenda, but she was

growing fond of the women in the sewing circle, and Mike and Christi had become good friends. It was a pleasure to be involved again, good to find a new community. She'd added cat food to her regular shop at Woolworths and the feral marmalade cat was dropping in a few times a week.

And then the levy was suddenly increased. The letter accompanying the new invoices explained that everything had become much more expensive.

"Sure it has," she said to Mike, waving the letter. "But not that much. 25%? Has Lenka's nail salon pushed up its prices by 25%?"

"That's a bit unfair," Mike said.

"It's her dress shop," Christi said. "She never wears the same thing twice. As for her shoes ..."

Outvoted, Mike gave in. He promised to secure an itemised budget – as chairman of the residents' association, he was entitled to see it.

It was a revelation. Mike and Myrna pored over the price the management was paying for landscaping – not too bad – roof repair – a bit high.

"By the way," Myrna added, "I'm not too good on construction costs. Are you? I'm just wondering if these prices are reasonable. For when they redo the cottages for the new buyers."

Mike worked it out per cottage per year. "They seem very high," Mike said. "But I'm not an expert. I have a friend who's a builder. Let's see what he says."

He was back the next day, shocked. "My friend couldn't believe how much we're paying," he said. "I have to admit, I had no idea."

One company did all the renovations. Myrna called her former firm, which looked up the directors. There was a familiar surname.

"Must be a relative of Lenka's," Mike said. "I'll ask her.

And I might have a word with the CEO."

A week later, the rate rise was rescinded, and replaced with a reasonable 8%. A month later, Riverends put out a call for companies to bid on renovating the cottages. Of course you go with people you trust. Lenka's brother's company might still win the contract, but he'd have to lower his prices.

As for Myrna, she'd made some progress with the marmalade cat.

She broached the subject one day while the cat was attacking a meal of Woolworths special salmon. "Would it be okay," she asked him, "if I brought a dog in?"

The cat looked up for a moment, then went back to the salmon. "What if it's a very small dog?" There was no response.

"I'll take that as a yes," she said. "Maybe I'll bring it up at the next meeting. You never know. I think I might be on a roll."

9

An ordinary Sunday

Palesa

It was an ordinary boring Sunday afternoon, with an ordinary forgettable Netflix action film playing – *Mad Max*, probably. Selwyn was nodding off and Palesa was making a shopping list – they were low on eggs and cos lettuce but Monday wasn't a good time to shop for either one; the spa was running low on essential oils, and she could order those online.

The door from the lounge to the stoep was open in the vain hope a breeze might enter. Instead, what crashed in was an armed gang of two – a giant, well over two metres, and a sidekick.

The giant demanded to know where the safe was hidden.

When she could speak, Palesa said "There is no safe."

"Shut up," said the giant. "Go back to your rooms. We'll deal with your master."

"Leave my wife alone," Selwyn said, starting to rise from his soft leather chair.

"Don't, Selwyn," she said.

"What's she doing here?" the giant said, looking puzzled. "They told me this was a white house."

The smaller intruder grabbed Palesa and as she pulled away, Selwyn attacked, but he was no competition for a young thug – or for the giant, who knocked him out with a pistol blow to the head.

Palesa crouched down next to Selwyn. "Why did you do that?" she asked, sounding, thinking about it later, rather shrill. "With your gun?"

"Tell me where the safe is. You people always have a safe."

"We people?" She looked up. "What are you talking about? Who are we people?"

"Shut up," he said, and the sidekick grabbed Palesa again, tried to pull her away.

"And let go of the girl. You're here to work. Where's the safe?" he said again.

"Didn't you hear me? There is no safe."

"I'll show you no safe," said the sidekick, and slapped her so hard her ears rang, then hit her in the mouth. "One two," he said.

"Maybe there's no safe," the giant said. "Okay, tie her up and get moving. You know what to do."

The young thug whipped Selwyn's woven belt off his unconscious body, tied Palesa's hands behind her back, and dragged her into the kitchen, throwing her against the dishwasher. He was pulling her jeans off and she was screaming "Get off me!" when the giant shouted "What are you up to in there? Get in here."

Twenty minutes later they'd unscrewed the flat screen television from the wall, gathered up laptops, iPads and cellphones and gone out the door with the keys to the Audi Selwyn had bought only a week before.

Selwyn was awake and calling for Palesa. Her mouth bleeding and her ears still ringing, she crawled to the panic button, managed to slide up the wall and pressed it with her shoulder. The belt was tight but she squeezed one hand out, breaking a small finger; the belt fell and she went back to Selwyn. When the security guards arrived, they found her with Selwyn's head in her lap, telling him softly that she was okay, nobody had hurt her. The guards called an ambulance.

Selwyn kept looking at Palesa, at her broken lips, the left side of her face beginning to swell. "It's all right," she told him, repeatedly. "Nobody hurt me. You're concussed and you're not seeing straight. Don't worry," repeating it until the ambulance arrived and the paramedics loaded Selwyn onto a stretcher and asked her what hospital to take him to.

Selwyn had remarked in the past on Palesa's tendency to drive too fast, and "He should see me now," she said grimly, pushing the Honda to the limit and arriving at the hospital before the ambulance. As she stood at the reception desk, fishing out her medical aid card, the ambulance driver told her about an accident they'd passed on the way to the house – an Audi crashed into the wall of the Alliance Française, a flat screen TV in the back, a giant last seen limping away towards Jan Smuts Avenue and a short guy running in the opposite direction. "Stupid asshole, didn't know how to drive is what the police think. Lucky he didn't wind up in the lake."

The spa was always closed on Monday. Palesa usually used the time to take inventory, chase suppliers and try to make sense of the paperwork required by the government's education and training authority. She had two young interns and liked to do things by the book, so she'd registered them there.

On this Monday, however, she spent the day chasing the doctors looking after Selwyn, who had been kept in for observation. On Tuesday he was allowed home, so she phoned her manager, Sophia, told her she'd probably be back the next day, and fetched him.

"You have to stop looking at my face," she told Selwyn on the way home. "I hope you've noticed that I'm driving very slowly."

"I heard you shouting," he said. "When I was supposed to be unconscious I heard you say 'Get off me'. Did they try to rape you?"

Palesa speeded up. "Nobody touched me," she said.

"It's a poor thing when a man can't protect his wife."

"Now you're being silly. Selwyn, I love you, but I don't need you to be my bodyguard. What did you want to do? They had guns."

"No matter. If I'd been faster ..."

"Then what? They could have killed you. They tried to kill you." She turned into their road. "They didn't try to kill me. They're not afraid of women." And then realised she shouldn't have reminded Selwyn, who said "No, they rape women. Are you sure ..."

"The subject is closed," she said, and stayed silent until they were inside the house. "The police will release the TV set and the laptops sooner or later. They said the car is a write-off."

Selwyn brightened up. "I'll just buy another one," he said.

That was not entirely out of character; Selwyn was a dentist who made a lot of money and spent it freely, although buying another new Audi before the insurance payout kicked in was perhaps excessive. Still, he needed a car.

He drove his new Audi home a week later – the same model but silver instead of white. "Actually, I prefer this one," he told Palesa. "A bit flashier. Not sedate. Silver. I prefer silver. And it has leather seats."

She was mixing a salad for dinner and paused, listening. Selwyn sounded ... not quite right. "The other one also had leather seats," she said.

"So it did," he said. "But these are nicer."

If he wanted to make the best of it, that was okay with her.

But there were changes that weren't okay. He started to worry when Palesa went to the salon. He'd phone from his surgery several times a day to see that she was all right.

At home, he arranged for heightened security, which was not a bad idea – not only beams that picked up movement but cameras everywhere, and he worried about what to do during load shedding. There was a backup battery, but batteries run out eventually.

On weekends, he wouldn't sit outside in the garden on his own, even though he kept one of the new panic buttons in a pocket. Four had been installed in various rooms, since Palesa had refused to carry one.

And he kept buying her gifts. First it was a Rolex. "I have a beautiful watch, Selwyn," she objected. "I wear it every day. You bought it for me two Christmases ago."

"But it wasn't a Rolex," he said.

A week later it was diamond earrings. She returned them. He brought home a Prada handbag. She returned that as well.

And then he stopped working.

Over the years, he'd turned a one-dentist operation into an industry: fancy offices, three dentists, a periodontist and two hygienists. His partners could take over his list, but what was he going to do all day if he didn't go to work?

He settled on worry. He would spend the day worrying, looking up crime statistics on the internet and phoning Palesa at the spa to see that she was still all right.

Palesa had problems of her own. Giving back was part of the ethos her parents had insisted upon. So was helping others climb the ladder of success. Lucky to be the daughter of schoolteachers, she should help others who hadn't been so fortunate. So she'd taken in two young women; in the end, the girls would have not only training but qualifications.

But she'd found one of the trainees pocketing expensive nail varnish – OPI, the best – to sell privately. Now what? Should she give her another chance or should she fire her? Monica wasn't the better of the two; Natalie was a star. Had it been Natalie, she would have simply given her a warning and sent her off to heat the wax for the next client. But

Monica – maybe she wasn't worth keeping.

The other problem also involved a young woman: their daughter Romy, who wanted to come home from London, where she was in her final year of a literature degree at London University's School of Oriental and African Studies. The year was nearly over and she'd had enough; she couldn't concentrate. All she could think about was the injury to her father and the pressure that left on her mother, and she was afraid they were both still in danger.

"I'm doing fine," Palesa said. "There's nothing to worry about. Nobody gets into this house who doesn't belong here. We have so many alarms and cameras it's ridiculous. We've got panic buttons all over the house. And CAP drives by every hour, and you know CAP – those guys carry guns. They're seriously tough. Do you know how lucky you are to be at SOAS? Finish the year. Then we'll talk about it. Your father's okay."

Palesa had to repeat this several times a week. Romy was beginning to sound like her father.

Selwyn was getting worse. He had begun prowling around the house in the middle of the night, setting off alarms. "What are you looking for?" Palesa asked sleepily, the first time it happened.

"Just testing," he said. "Back to bed, my darling."

She learned to ignore the alarms; the security company phoned each time, Selwyn told them it was a mistake, and basically Palesa wasn't needed.

And then one night two months after the robbery he fell, wandering in the dark. He cried out in such pain that Palesa woke and panicked. She was reluctant to call their house doctor at three in the morning, so she summoned an ambulance, followed it to Milpark emergency, and found, as dawn was breaking, that Selwyn had cracked three ribs, would stay a day or two to be sure that was the only damage, and they'd let her know when she could fetch him.

"I don't know what to do," she told their doctor later that morning. "He's not right, Glenn. The robbery really threw him."

"Let me know when you bring him home, and I'll come by," Glenn said.

Selwyn was released the next day. Palesa settled him down, made his lunch – smoked salmon, capers, rye bread and a glass of prosecco – and Glenn stopped in on the way home from his rooms. They had a long talk – close to an hour – and when he emerged, Glenn looked worried.

"He's in a lot of pain, and there's nothing we can do about it, Palesa," he said. "Cracked ribs have to heal on their own. They've given him some very strong pain pills so they should help, but watch him – the pills might make him even more erratic."

"He's going to get better," Palesa said.

"I hope so," Glenn said, then caught himself. "Of course he will. And when he's better may I suggest counselling? He kept returning to the same subject. That he'd failed you as a husband when the rapist –"

"There was no rapist. There was no rape. There was a robbery."

"Yes. I understand. I'm not sure he understands. He said you were punched in the mouth."

"Yes. And? He was pistol-whipped."

"He doesn't see it that way. Just ... phone me if there's any change at all. I'm five minutes away."

The next morning she was relieved to find Selwyn had not wandered off but was awake and smiling, lying next to her. She went off to make the coffee.

"I missed this in hospital," he said, when she handed him a cup. "You make the best coffee. The best."

Uh-oh. Palesa's coffee was ordinary because she was

basically a tea drinker. "Can I make you breakfast?" she asked, brightly.

"Not yet. Just sit here, with me," he said. "Let's call Romy."

"It's a bit early in London."

"In an hour. Will it be too early in an hour?"

"She'll be here tomorrow. You can talk to her then." The academic year was virtually over and Romy had booked to come home. Palesa was quietly relieved; the pressure of handling everything on her own was getting to her.

"Let me wish her a safe flight," he said.

An hour later, she phoned. Romy was packing.

"Your father wants a word," Palesa said.

"How is Dad? What did the doctor say?"

"Ask him," she said, and handed Selwyn the phone.

"How's my girl?" His voice was strange – slow, listless, a little slurred. Maybe too many pain pills. "A first? They said? My baby I'm proud of you. Remember that." He handed Palesa the phone.

"Why did you tell her to remember that? She'll be home tomorrow. She won't forget it." She kissed Selwyn on the forehead, and then took the phone. "Romy, I need to know when your plane is coming in so I can pick you up." There was a pause. "I know there are Ubers but let's be safe. There are a lot of dodgy people hanging around the airport." Romy pointed out that nobody ever picked her up at Heathrow and she was just fine, but Palesa insisted.

Selwyn had been holding Palesa's free hand throughout the conversation – she'd had to put the phone down to reach for a pad of paper and a pen to write down Romy's flight number when, as usual, she won the battle with her daughter.

She had pressed speakerphone and was writing Romy's flight details when Selwyn squeezed her hand, kissed it, and let it go. When she turned around, he was asleep.

He never woke up.

§

They'd met when Palesa, who had come to Johannesburg from the West Rand to study for a B.Com degree, thought it a good idea to find a gym, a general practitioner and a dentist. A fellow student had recommended Selwyn.

Selwyn had examined Palesa's teeth and said "I'm not going to make any money from this mouth," and smiled. She'd laughed – and they'd taken it from there.

It had been an interesting marriage, combining two cultures with very little friction. Palesa's parents had had to talk Selwyn out of paying lobola; and when the odd cousin or niece – or, once, her brother – moved in, because the biggest house in the best area was now an alternative family home, Selwyn made no objection.

For her part, Palesa learned the ways of Selwyn's background. He was not religious, but it made no difference; there was a culture he'd been raised in and she was surprised to discover it was not very different from her own. However distant the relative, members of extended families were still family. Children were there to be cherished. Education came first.

And in times of need, the community took over.

She phoned Glenn, who phoned the Chevrah Kadisha, and by the time Romy's plane landed – she took an Uber after all – the funeral had been arranged, a rabbi found and a list of mourners contacted. All that remained was to rank the pallbearers. Palesa's father and brother were in the first group; Selwyn's partners and Romy's boyfriend were in the second.

What? Romy had a boyfriend? Why didn't Palesa know that?

Romy couldn't stop crying, which irritated Palesa, who wanted her support; but Palesa's mother stepped in, holding on to both of them throughout the long, winding walk to the burial site; the brief graveside service; and the terrible moment when the mourners began shovelling the red earth piled next to the grave onto the coffin, the first few shovels of Johannesburg's red clay landing with a thud.

Then it was over. Twenty-five years, gone. Just like that.

"Don't think about it now," her mother said. "Your father and I will stay as long as you need us."

Palesa leaned against her mother in the back seat of her father's car, grateful that Romy had gone off in her boyfriend's car. Once home, she looked around at what now seemed vaguely unfamiliar; thanked her parents and her brother for coming; asked her mother to look after Romy; went into the bedroom, closed the door and went to sleep – a healing sleep that continued until the next morning, when her mother hauled her out of bed.

"Feeling better?" she asked.

Palesa thought about it. "Feeling nothing," she said finally.

"I think you need tea. And we must talk."

Palesa nodded. "Half an hour," she said. "I need a bath."

The tea was ready as Palesa emerged. As her father went out for a walk up to the shops, her mother poured the tea. "You have a spa to manage," she said. "You have a home to run. And you have to heal your relationship with your daughter."

Was it that obvious? "There's nothing wrong with my relationship with Romy. What did she say?"

"She didn't need to say anything. I could see it. Where is she now?"

"How would I know? I've been asleep."

"Precisely. In many ways." She paused, letting it sink in. "Your father and I will stay as long as you need us. I think

126

you need us now. There is a great deal of paperwork when a person passes. Certificates. Bills. Sympathy cards to answer. You shouldn't have to do it on your own and Romy has disappeared. When can we start?"

"I'm not doing anything at the moment. Should we have breakfast first? I assume you've done a spreadsheet."

"Of course."

"Good. Let's have a look."

It took the rest of the week to get things squared away. Two days after the funeral, Palesa and her father met with the family lawyer, who handed them the papers they needed – everything from multiple copies of the death certificate to a certificate from the Master of the High Court appointing Palesa an executor of her husband's estate.

Romy arrived late on Friday afternoon. Palesa's parents withdrew, leaving Palesa and Romy alone in the house.

"So. You've come home. Where did you disappear to, by the way? I could have used some help here," Palesa said.

"You don't need me. You don't need anybody. I'm exhausted," Romy said and went into her room. Palesa heard the key turn in the lock.

Okay, no mother-daughter reunion, no chance of sorting things out. Might as well go back to work.

Which she did, on Friday, to find the spa in chaos. There were piles of paperwork, the appointment book was a mess – how had three women been booked at the same time for the same apprentice? – and when she checked the supplies, there were gaps unaccounted for. Why was she paying Sophia an assistant manager's salary?

"We have very few wax strips left. What's happened to them?" she asked Sophia, who said she had no idea.

"It's not the first time. Where's Monica?"

"I don't know," Sophia said. "She never came in yesterday."

"Did you try to contact her?"

"She's useless, Palesa. I don't care if she goes."

"Well I care if she goes with our entire supply of wax. I don't know how she thinks she's going to heat it. And quite a lot of nail varnish has gone. Again. I can't afford to lose so much of it."

"Is there so much missing?"

"Don't you check the stock? Don't you see what the girls walk away with?"

Sophia stared at Palesa and then she started to cry. Howling, she ran into the changeroom.

Palesa just shook her head. Three women booked for the same treatment with the same girl at the same time. At least Natalie was there. She'd take one of them and Sophia would just have to stop howling and take the third. She headed for the change-room.

§

It was close to 8pm by the time Palesa pulled into the garage. It had been an exhausting, irritating day. How long had it been since she'd derived any pleasure from running the business on her own?

Romy was in the kitchen, putting plates in the dishwasher. "Did you go to work?" she asked, by way of greeting.

"I did," Palesa said. "The spa was a mess."

"How could you do that? Poppa's only been dead a week."

"And what would staying home accomplish?"

"It would show some respect. You're supposed to be in mourning."

"And you think I'm not?" Palesa was irritated but she was also hungry. She opened the refrigerator and poked around in the vegetable drawer.

"It's hard to tell with you. You're always working. It's all about money with you."

Palesa had had enough. "How dare you judge me?" she said, turning around, her voice raised. "Who's going to pay for the food you just ate? Who pays rates on this house so you have somewhere to live? Tell me that."

Romy banged the dishwasher shut. "You never let me come home when I wanted to. If I'd come home after the robbery Poppa would still be alive" – and the tears started.

Palesa was too shocked to be insulted. "Your father died of a stroke. Read Glenn's note. There's no way you could have prevented that."

"Glenn would say anything you wanted him to say."

"I'll be sure to tell him what you think of him the next time he saves your life," Palesa said. "Why don't you go to your room, or your boyfriend, whoever he is. I don't really care where you go. Just leave me alone."

Palesa was too tired for this. She had not eaten since breakfast, but the exchange with Romy had taken what little energy she had left. She sat at the breakfast table, her head in her hands, and soon fell asleep.

Hours later, Romy nudged her awake and slid a cup of tea towards her left hand.

"I'm sorry, Mommy," she said. "I guess that wasn't fair. Glenn wouldn't make things up."

"Is that all?"

"Why, is there more?"

Not worth the hassle. "No, my darling," Palesa said. "Why don't you make me an omelette and we can talk about it. I'm starving."

The truce lasted until the next morning, when Romy wandered into the kitchen, still in pyjamas, as Palesa – dressed for work – was finishing her coffee.

"There's oatmeal on the stove," Palesa said. "It's good for lowering cholesterol. Your father's family has a genetic predisposition to high cholesterol. I don't suppose you've ever checked yours."

"Thanks Mommy," Romy said, and began dishing up.

"Have you?"

"Have I what?"

"Ever checked your cholesterol?"

No answer. A new tack required.

"Who's the boyfriend?"

That got Romy's attention. "Dominick. His name's Dominick."

"Have you known him long? You're hardly ever here."

"London," Romy said, emptying the remains of the honey into her porridge.

"That's a lot of sugar," Palesa said, then wondered why she'd bothered.

"We came back on the same plane. We shared the Uber. He's getting a PhD if he ever finishes his thesis."

"Did you know him in London?"

"I just said, Mommy. What else do you need to know? Am I sleeping with him? Not at the moment. Does he have any money? I have no idea. Who's his family? How would I know?"

Palesa gave up and left for work.

It was not a refuge. Monica came back, and when Palesa asked her where the nail varnish had gone she screamed at her. "You always blame me! Okay, once. Not this time."

Sophia took that moment to announce she had a terrible hacking cough and was going to the doctor, which changed the dynamics considerably: now Palesa needed Monica. "I'll try to believe you," she said. "Just don't do it again. Please take Mrs van Niekerk in Room Three. A full body massage with, let's see, neroli oil. Here's her card."

The day didn't improve – there was the client who showed up with very bad flu. Palesa asked her to go home and come back when she was better, and she was furious, managing to spit out "black bitch" as she waltzed through the door. Which was puzzling, since she was also black – and also a bitch, always complaining, never satisfied. Palesa was crossing her name off the appointment book as Sophia phoned to say the doctor had booked her off until Tuesday.

Natalie, the star intern, had a client in Room Two and a new client who had come early was in reception, paging through magazines. She was booked for a facial, nothing hectic – but when Natalie's client screamed she stood up, alarmed. "I think I'd better go," she said.

"The client has come for a wax," Palesa said. "Sometimes it can be uncomfortable."

"Sounds like she's being murdered. Sorry. Maybe another time," she said, and left.

Saturday was always a busy day, but with two cancellations Palesa could get some orders in and bills paid. After the last customer left and the girls had cleaned the treatment rooms, she sat at the desk for a good half hour, thinking about selling up. And doing what?

She wasn't looking forward to going home, to a sullen Romy, but she needn't have worried. Romy wasn't there. Instead there was a note on the kitchen table. It read:

Sitting in the garden
Listen to the lions roar.
Isn't Parkview lekker?

She had to smile. As a small child, Romy always said she could hear the lions roaring. Palesa said she was dreaming, the sound didn't travel that far from the Zoo, but Selwyn backed Romy up. "Elephants too," he would say. "And hyaenas. What noisy animals," and Romy would laugh.

What had happened to our happy little family? She decided

not to think about it. That was long over.

Romy seemed to have moved out. When Palesa went into her room, she saw her cosmetics gone – those were the first things she looked for – and some of her clothes. Okay. Maybe she'll come back. Or maybe not.

The next note came on WhatsApp:

Dusk is on its way
Time to pour the sundowners
And check the alarms.

Palesa could have WhatsApped back "Where the hell are you?" but she knew this was not the way to deal with the new, independent Romy, whose link to the family seemed to have been seriously frayed by the death of her father.

Instead, she wrote "I love your poetry. What is it?"

There came a long explanation – it was called a haiku and was a Japanese form among many Japanese literary forms Romy had studied at SOAS. She'd fallen in love with the comic-book art called manga, which had led her to Japanese art and literature and the language, which was a major reason she'd gone to SOAS. The private tutor Selwyn had arranged in Johannesburg was only able to take her so far.

"Should I try to write one?" Palesa wrote. And there was silence.

The problems at the spa carried on. One of her free-lance staff announced she'd been diagnosed with tuberculosis and would have to be booked off for six months, her full wages paid. "I don't think so," Palesa said, planning to consult a lawyer. When the girl – who was a manicurist – left, so did quite a lot of expensive nail varnish.

Palesa felt guilty for blaming Monica, sought her out and apologised. Monica said she understood and her boyfriend was outside and could she leave early? "Of course," Palesa said. It was a slow day. She watched as Monica climbed into an S-Class Mercedes.

It was two weeks later that the next note arrived from Romy:

Scattered on the pavement
All my trash spread out to view
Recyclers have been.

That gave no clue about where Romy had disappeared to – there was trash all over Johannesburg's pavements, even in Parkview, when the recyclers sorted through rubbish before the Pikitup trucks arrived. But a couple of days later, this one appeared on Palesa's phone:

Colour on the pavement
Half-rolled purple condom dropped
Someone's feeling good.

She had to smile. Romy was getting her sense of humour back. Then hours later, this one:

Breaking into cars
Spotted by the street committee
Beaten to a pulp.

It was time to worry, but she'd have to be careful. "Romy, I barely met your young man at the funeral, and he was so helpful there. I would love to thank him properly," she wrote. "Will you bring Dominick to lunch on Sunday?"

"What's on the menu?" Romy wrote back.

"Coq au vin?" Palesa wrote. "Or lasagna?"

"We're vegetarian now," Romy wrote.

That was easy. "I'll do a vegetable curry," she said. As

there was no reply, she assumed they would show up – and they did.

When she saw Dominick, she remembered him from the funeral – vaguely, but most of what she remembered from that terrible day was vague. He was tall, skinny and blond, and he never looked her in the eye. His manner of speaking was offhand and appeared to consist of single words or unfinished sentences: "Yes and no but sometimes we were …" was his response to "So did you grow up around here?" and "Maybe. Sometimes" was the response to "I've thought about becoming a vegetarian. Romy used to complain that we ate too many salads. It must be difficult when you go out to eat."

She was dying to know if he had a job. "Romy told me you're a PhD candidate. In Japanese?"

"You could say that," he said – impressive, an entire sentence.

"Will you go to work at the embassy then?" she asked, ignoring Romy's glare.

"Maybe," he said. "Somewhere."

Romy looked shocked. "Where?" she asked him, presumably forgetting her mother was listening avidly.

"Oh anywhere," he said. "Haven't thought much."

"But I don't want to leave my job," Romy said.

Palesa held her breath, but there was no more information forthcoming, so she went into the kitchen to fetch the dessert. As she was carrying the tarte tatin back out to the stoep, she heard Romy say "I'll never find a job like that in Italy."

Then she arrived, and they dropped the subject.

Okay, she thought, after they left, this much she knew: Romy had a job she liked. Dominick had no plans. They lived in a neighbourhood that had street committees. Oh my God. She had briefly thought of following Dominick's car at a discreet distance to find out where Romy was staying but was afraid she'd be spotted. Detective work was not part of her skill set.

And diplomacy seemed to be deserting her too. On Tuesday, Monica asked for a discreet meeting, which happened around four, when the last client had left.

"Here's the thing," Monica said. "My boyfriend has a lot of money and he'll back me."

"Good," Palesa said. "Back you in what?"

"Oh didn't I say? I want to buy your spa."

"You?" The tone was not diplomatic. "What do you know about running a spa?"

"I know a lot. I've watched you. Why, do you think I can't do it?"

"Do you know how long I studied cosmetology? Three years, fulltime. After my business degree. You've only been doing this for a year."

"Okay then, what about a partnership?" She looked out the window at the front, where the Merc was idling.

"You're not ready, Monica," Palesa said. "I don't want to see you crash and burn out. You have promise but you don't know enough."

"That's what you think," Monica said, and moved towards the door. "If you don't want to do it I'll find another salon to buy. You're not the only show in town."

Actually what Palesa had said wasn't entirely what she thought. In her view, Monica would always be mediocre. She didn't pay enough attention to detail and her mind tended to wander at unfortunate times, forgetting she'd left a client with her feet wrapped in hot wax or painting over a nail she'd just painted.

There was another haiku on the dining room table. Romy must have come to take more of her clothes. This one held no clues:

Someone's wrapping trees
Cloth of silver, red and gold
Jo'burg's full of loonies.

For a month, Monica was absent at least two mornings a week – presumably looking for a spa to buy. Meanwhile Romy was emailing increasingly worrying haikus, for example:

Paying for your parking
Girl behind you briefly trips
Whoops - your phone is gone.

And

Women shouting "Vimba"
5am! What's all the noise?
Caught another thief.

With that one, Palesa could stand the mystery no longer. She phoned Romy – and, to her surprise, Romy answered.

"Can we talk?" Palesa said.

"Yes," Romy said, "but not now. I'm on a deadline. I'll phone you later."

She didn't, but when Palesa walked into her kitchen hours later, there she was, making coffee. "Tea?" she asked.

"Thanks," Palesa said, and leaned against a counter. "Staying for dinner?"

Romy shook her head. "You sounded worried this morning," she said. "I'm not pregnant again."

"I didn't think you were. It's your poetry. It's sounding hectic. I need to know. You're my only, precious child. I need to know you're all right."

Romy covered the teapot with a tea towel. "I have a job,"

she said, poured her coffee and turned her back to fetch the milk from the refrigerator.

"With deadlines. We all have deadlines, I suppose. What kind of job?"

"I'm an editor. No, not an editor. I'm a junior editor. Making peanuts but I love the work. And they may publish my poetry."

"Oh Romy I'm so proud of you!" Palesa said, and moved to hug her, but Romy was pouring milk into a jug. "Your father would be so happy."

"Yes. Better than the abortion."

"He never knew," Palesa said.

"I don't believe you." Romy slammed the jug down on the counter. "How could you resist telling him?"

"And break his heart?"

Romy stared at her. "Why did he think I was bleeding to death?"

"I told him it was not his concern, it was a female issue. He never asked. Oh my God, Romy, you could have died. Those back-street pills – if it hadn't been for Glenn, taking charge. He said he got you to the hospital just in time."

"Maybe Poppa didn't want to know. But I think he knew." She poured her mother's tea, added a drop of milk, handed it over, and asked "How's the spa going?"

Palesa was surprised at Romy's interest, but answered honestly: "It's more trouble than it's worth. One of the interns wants to buy it. Maybe I should let her."

"You can't do that." Romy looked appalled. "What will you do next?"

"Do I have to do anything next?"

They drank, leaning against the cupboards. Finally, Palesa asked: "Do you make enough money to live on? Do you need help?"

"Dominick's family has mega-bucks," Romy said.

"But he's probably going to leave," Palesa said.

"What gave you that idea? If he goes, I go with him."

"And give up your dream job?"

"No," Romy said. "He's not going."

Palesa pushed her luck. "Where are you living?"

"Don't worry about it," Romy said, put her cup down and left. Outside, she was on the phone, and three minutes later an Uber showed up.

If she'd been living in a spy novel, Palesa could have taken the Toyota's licence number, traced the driver and forced him to tell her where he'd taken her daughter. But she was living in a world where nobody told anybody anything – certainly not middle-aged, middle-class businesswomen. So she'd have to be satisfied with what she'd learned: that Romy was employed, that her relationship with Dominick was shaky, and that she still cared enough to come home when she thought her mother was worried about her.

That was enough for the moment.

The next day, both her interns resigned. They'd found a small salon for Monica's boyfriend to buy. Palesa insisted they work out their notice, but although Natalie showed up, Monica was gone. It meant a pile of paperwork for the government training authority, looking for replacements, testing and training ... it was a terrible month.

Meanwhile, Romy kept sending haikus. The first one was light:

Red and itchy eyes
Sounds of sneezing, wheezing, coughing
Harbingers of spring.

But just after Palesa had chosen two junior employees – no more trainees, it was too much hassle – there was another, darker haiku:

Dead rats everywhere
Sticky paper, chocolate smears
Rotting in the sun.

It was a cry for help – and there was nothing Palesa could do. Romy didn't answer her phone. She didn't know where Romy was living or where she was employed – but she knew she worked for a publisher, and that was a start.

It took ten phone calls before she hit the right one. Romy hadn't been to work for a couple of days. She'd phoned in sick and was told she'd have to bring a doctor's note. Palesa asked if they had an address. The woman on the line asked who wanted to know, and when she heard it was Romy's mother, said "Well, we have an address in Parkview."

So: a dead end.

But the next day, Palesa had a call from a woman who said she was Romy's landlady and suggested she come and pick her up. "A lovely girl and a nice boyfriend," she said, "but he's been gone for two weeks and I don't think she can pay the rent. They didn't pay much last month. I don't think she's eating – I brought her soup last night and she ate like a starving child. I'm not sure she's all right."

The address was in Yeoville. Palesa drove through potholed, rubbish-strewn streets, dodging cars too big for the narrow roads, stopping finally in front of a semi-detached house where, magically, there was no rubbish, no graffiti, nobody sitting on the steps smoking dope, although there were a few dodgy guys hanging around the spaza shop up the road.

As they walked down a corridor, past closed doors, the landlady said she'd found Palesa's number on Romy's phone, under "Mom". Romy was in what must once have been a lounge – there was an ornate fireplace at one end. The room was immaculate but barely furnished: a single bed, a wardrobe, a table with a two-burner hotplate and two chairs. Romy was slumped in one, reading.

"I need you," Palesa said, and Romy turned around. "I'm having a terrible time at the spa and I can't bear living without Selwyn. Please, Romy. Come home. I need my child."

As she said it, she realised it was true. So did Romy, who – without a word – pulled her suitcase out of the wardrobe. The landlady helped to shove Romy's clothes into the suitcase and carried it out to the car.

Palesa forced Romy back to work the next day. There was no doctor's note but she didn't lose her job – poets were allowed some leeway in the matter of mental health.

For the next two months, Palesa monitored the new girls at the spa. None of the supplies went missing, which was a plus, and there was only one complaint – from the usual client who always found something to moan about but kept coming back.

Eventually Romy agreed to try out the new girls. She reported back that they thought Palesa was firm, but mostly fair, and they thought Romy should teach her mother a bit of tact.

"They also think you should add a boutique. You know, accessories, scarves, T-shirts, and things like that."

"And who would run it? I don't have the time. Are you interested?"

Romy looked amazed. "No, Mom. I'm a poet, not a merchant. Don't you want to extend your range of expertise? Get into something new? You know, fashion?"

A poet, not a merchant. Okay. Said with just a touch of dismissiveness.

Would a book of Romy's haikus be accepted? Hard to predict, but on the night Palesa found a new haiku on the dining room table, she knew Romy was now okay:

Rain is pelting down
Small rat runs for grapevine shelter
Orphan in the storm.

The workshop

Harry

The call came in the middle of poker night.

Claire had urged Harry to go. The pain was gone and she was feeling so well that she'd arranged to pop in for tea with her new friend next door.

Poker night was the second and fourth Tuesday of the month, had been for 40 years. Harry must keep up his traditions, even though they'd moved out of the neighbourhood, she said. He must go and enjoy himself.

They'd been playing for two hours when Harry's phone rang in the pocket of his jacket, draped carefully over the back of his chair.

"Just turn the damned thing off," Clinton said, irritated. He was the host and his wife Hilda was in the kitchen making too much noise as she prepared the eats.

But Harry didn't have such a brilliant hand, so he answered, and in that moment, his life froze.

When Claire's new friend had carried in the tea and biscuits, she'd found Claire had slid to the floor. She phoned the care centre – that was the point of living in a retirement village, help was on hand – but when the paramedics got there half an hour later, there was nothing they could do.

So the centre phoned Harry.

He folded and headed for the door.

"And where do you think you're going?" Clinton asked. "If you need the toilet, you know where it is."

"Claire's dead," Harry said, and left.

It had been Claire's idea to sell their house and move to a retirement village. Both their children were abroad, Jeffrey in California and Arlene in Sydney. The house was too big for an ageing couple, and the stairs were a problem for Claire, who was due for a hip replacement.

"No," he'd said. "Bad idea. You can go to a retirement village but I'm not going anywhere."

Claire had visited a number of retirement homes anyway, signed them up on two waiting lists and in what she was told was record time – one year! – they were offered a deal too good to pass up. Especially as an estate agent had promised to sell their house for at least ten times what they'd paid for it. The children urged Harry to go ahead and sell and to move into the lovely cottage in the retirement village. It was smaller than their house but more manageable, with an adjacent two-car garage, an expansive lawn in front and a walled garden in the back.

Harry finally gave in. The house was sold and though when they factored in inflation it went for only three times, not ten times, what they'd paid for it, it was still a reasonable windfall.

He suspected that the real reason Claire and the children were so insistent on the move was their concern for his health. He'd had a small stroke. That's why it was ironic that Claire was the one who'd had a heart attack, only a week after they'd moved in.

They delayed the funeral until Jeffrey and Arlene could get to Johannesburg, leaving their various partners and children behind, since the flights were long, arduous and expensive.

The funeral was predictably awful. Jeffrey spoke glowingly, Arlene couldn't stop sobbing, the rabbi had never met any of the family and the plot they were given was so far Harry had to take the minibus supplied to transport disabled and elderly mourners.

Afterwards they had gone to Clinton's for tea and cakes. "Prayers?" Hilda asked. "Tonight and tomorrow night? We can have them here."

"No prayers," Harry said. He sat silent for a moment, then said "Thanks. But no thanks."

Arlene, who had at last stopped sobbing, wanted to sit shivah for at least a day or two, if not the prescribed seven days. Harry told her that she could sit shivah in Sydney, but to leave him in peace.

The children loved the cottage, although they stayed in an AirBnB and not in the extra bedroom that Harry didn't need. They left two days after the funeral, making Harry promise to visit them. They both said they'd Uber to the airport, but Harry was of the generation that considered taxis a copout, so he drove first Arlene and then, hours later, Jeffrey, to the airport, waved them off and returned to the cottage.

And then he closed the door.

For the first few days, he slept, waking only for meals – the odd chop or steak from the freezer, a baked potato, nothing much. Now and again he could hear someone ringing his doorbell, but he ignored it. A ringing phone was an irritating intrusion so he ignored that too.

Sleeping was a good idea, because when he was awake he was angry – angry that Claire had trapped him in a place he didn't want to be and then left him there on his own. He had not lived alone since his marriage a good 45 years before, yet here he was, dumped amid alien corn.

But he could sleep only so long. After a week, on his way to the kitchen to see if anything was left in the freezer, he passed the bookcase and remembered that they had not been there long enough to sort through the books. So after microwaving a cottage pie from Woolworths – the last of the emergency rations Arlene had stowed in the freezer – he began arranging the books they had brought.

Harry was a linguist of sorts. He'd discovered an ability to absorb languages on the first trip abroad he and Claire had taken together. Claire had been completely bamboozled by street signs in Barcelona, but Harry found them easy to decipher, and from there, learning the language – and then other languages – had been a hobby.

He had books in Spanish, French, Italian and his latest interest, Zulu. He'd toyed with the idea of learning Mandarin, but in the end the prospect of learning a tonal language written in pictographs did not appeal. Besides, Zulu was more useful. He had no intention of travelling to China but he lived in a country where, out of 11 official languages, Zulu rivaled English as the lingua franca. It would be useful to understand what people were saying about him.

Arranging the books kept him occupied most of a day and he took a book of French poetry to bed.

The next morning, he ordered supplies from Woolworths, online – meat, mostly, and potatoes, eggs, bread, and the same frozen dinners Arlene had laid in for emergencies. They promised a delivery that afternoon.

What to do when there's nothing to do? He walked through the rooms looking for work, and found it in the second bedroom. There was his latest schooner in a bottle.

Harry had learned how to build ships in bottles in his teens, and had forgotten it by his mid-twenties. But when retirement loomed he'd bought what he'd needed, set up a workshop in the garage and begun building a delicate sea-going structure to insert into a narrow-necked bottle. He'd completed it a month before the move.

He carried the schooner into the living room, placed it on the coffee table and gazed at it for a while before making himself a cup of tea. He thought about going outside and taking a walk – that's what people talked about when they heard where he was going, the wonderful paths through the woods – but was afraid he'd run into someone so he stayed put.

"This is a terrible place," he said to Claire when she finally convinced him to look at the cottage, at least. "You never see anybody."

"How do you know?"

"We haven't seen anybody yet and we've been here for 20 minutes. Nobody lives here."

"That should suit you," she said. "You never like seeing people anyway."

Almost on cue, the doorbell rang. It was too early for the Woolworths delivery, so he walked into the walled garden outside, missing the piece of paper slipped under the front door.

He found it a little while later. "Poker tomorrow night," it read. "@Clinton's." As if it were ever anywhere else.

He crumpled up the note, found a book and went back into the garden to read in the sun.

It was late afternoon when the Woolworths guy rang his doorbell. He took a chance and opened the door, and there was the chap with – presumably – what he'd ordered. He signed for the packages, took them into the kitchen and returned, digging in his pocket for a tip. As the guy turned away, Harry started to close the door.

But he wasn't fast enough. A tall elderly man had moved with incredible speed towards his cottage.

"Just a minute, young fellow," the man said. "My wife has sent me over with a cake." He held it out. Harry had no choice but to take it.

"Not a bad place," said the guy. "I'm Derek, by the way. I live over the road." He peered into the living room. "That's interesting. Your ship in a bottle – what a remarkable feat. I've long wondered how it works. What do you call it?"

"The Busted Flush," said Harry.

Derek laughed. "I'm not that ignorant," he said. "The Busted Flush was a yacht, not a schooner. John D Macdonald, wasn't it? Travis McGee. Took his retirement in installments. Not like us. I used to read all those books back in the seventies. Where did you come by the schooner?"

Harry was flabbergasted – not only because he was having a conversation with an old guy who'd forced his way into the cottage, but also that he was discovering another fan of the thriller series. Those books must have been out of print for decades.

"Actually," he said, "I built it."

Derek walked past Harry to peer closely at the ship. "Superb craftsmanship," he said. "What is that, teak?"

"The hull is teak. The deck is mahogany."

"And the sails? How do you get the ship into the bottle?"

"Carefully. It's not difficult, once you know how."

Derek peered at the bottle for a minute more and then, thankfully, moved towards the door. "Here's an idea," he said, standing just inside, so Harry had to listen. "Some of us have set up a workshop down by the coffee shop. You know where the coffee shop is."

Harry didn't know where the coffee shop was, nor did he want to know.

"Won't you come down and show us how it's done? Maybe do some work down there? We have some stellar equipment. Some of it we leave bolted to the workbench for anyone to use. These cottages aren't equipped for woodworking. You'd have to move your car out of the garage."

Harry said he'd think about it, and when Derek finally left, and he could close the door, he managed to forget about it.

But Derek didn't. When Harry walked into the living room the next morning on his way to the kitchen, someone – he assumed Derek – had slid a map under the door, with an arrow pointing to the workshop.

§

Hilda was all smiles and support when Harry showed up for poker that night.

"So what's it like living there? You know, Clinton, we could do worse. Maybe we should put our names down."

"I'll go when I have to, and I don't have to," Clinton said.

"Have you met anybody yet? I bet all the women are leaving cakes and casseroles on your doorstep."

"Are there women there? I haven't seen any," Harry said.

"Sit down, Harry. Are we here to play cards or to talk? That means you, Hilda."

She smiled and exited.

The cards weren't working so well for him that night. He lost a bundle.

"Hell, you can afford it," Clinton said, as Hilda brought in the eats.

Harry had to acknowledge it was true. He had no one to spend money on but himself anymore. No reason to get up in the morning either, but that was his own business.

He speared a herring rollmop but it slid off his fork and bounced onto his thigh, leaving a smear, before falling onto the carpet.

He shook his head. "Don't know how that happened," he said. "Got a cloth? I'll clean it up."

But Hilda was there already. She handed a damp cloth to Harry. "You'd better take care of that," she said, "or you'll smell like herring for months." She waited while he followed her instructions, then took the cloth and knelt down to scrub the spot on the carpet.

"Let me do that," he said.

"Forget it. She's younger than you are," Clinton said. "And she goes to yoga. Don't you, darling? Every day."

"Not every day," she said, smiling and scrubbing at the

carpet. "Often."

"What are we all now, 70? 71? Shaun. You're the old man here. 75?"

"73," Shaun said. "You know what they say. After 70, when you bend down to tie your shoe, you have to aim."

That got a laugh out of Clinton – short, loud and raucous. "Shoes, you say? That's not all you've got to aim at. Am I right, Hilda?"

This time she started to blush. She disappeared into the kitchen.

"Find yourself a nice woman at that retirement village, Harry. Worth their weight ..."

Harry smiled, ruefully. These were friends he'd known all his life, played poker with every fortnight, except when he and Claire took the kids to the Kruger Park or once, to Mauritius. Or when he and Claire travelled to Europe, after the kids had grown, and gone. Italy – that was the best. Claire loved Italy.

Harry had zero interest in finding a nice woman. Or in anything else.

Back at the cottage an hour later, he picked up the bottle with the schooner. Not bad, he thought. Maybe he should try something a bit more challenging. A catamaran? He smiled at the thought of getting two hulls through a narrow bottleneck, picked a new Italian bestseller out of the bookcase, poured himself a brandy and settled in to read.

§

He was in bed at 8am on Monday when Derek rang the bell.

"I see you're a late sleeper," he said when Harry opened the door. "I'm up with the birds. Never mind, the workshop's open at eight but the chaps only start coming in around nine. Can I trouble you for a cup of tea? My good wife is still asleep."

When Harry brought out the tea – and a cup of coffee for himself – Derek had made himself at home on the couch, turning the schooner this way and that.

"I can't see how you did that," he said. "Will you bring it to the workshop? Show the chaps how it works?"

There was no escape. Okay, he'd humour the old guy, but only once. And he had to stop answering the door.

They were on their way, the ship safely encased in bubble wrap in a cardboard box, when Derek said "Oh by the way there's a fellow there says he knows you."

"Oh?"

"Didn't catch his name. Well, I did catch it but then I dropped it." He chuckled. "You know how it is, at this age we can't remember where we left the keys."

Harry thought about turning around and going back to the flat. He always remembered where he left the keys. And people's names. And their faces. Is this what it's like living in a retirement village, engaging with the other residents?

"Don't stop, we're not there yet," Derek said. "Not far. Got a stone in your shoe?"

The workshop was an enormous space. "Used to be a storehouse. They kept the broken chairs in here until the coffee shop got a man in to repair them. Paint, old curtains, you name it, they just piled it in here. We cleaned it out, brought in our equipment."

It was a woodworker's dream: saws, both radial and table; planers, drills, lathes, grinders, sanders ... Harry couldn't take it all in.

"The most important piece of equipment here is over there." Derek indicated a Nespresso machine. "Did I get you out of bed? Have another coffee."

One man was making pull toys. Another was sawing narrow planks, and a third was sanding ... something. Hard to tell what it was, but his face looked vaguely familiar. He looked up, saw Harry and stopped what he was doing.

"Harry!" he said, coming over. "I can't believe it!" He turned to Derek. "This guy is a genius with sneezewood. You wouldn't believe the xylophones we made. We couldn't stop sneezing. It was great wood, though."

"Hello, Rodney," Harry said. "What are you making over there?"

"That's all you've got to say?" He turned to Derek. "I last saw this guy 40 years ago. You know?" He said, turning back to Harry, "you don't look all that different."

"You always were a lousy liar."

"That's the old Harry. Remember the VW bus? Belonged to Colin? Long dead now ... the VW, not Colin. At least I don't think so. You and the other guys never let me talk to the cops. They'd see through me in a minute."

"Those VW buses didn't do any speed at all," Derek said. "What interest did the boys in blue take in a bus that – I believe its highest speed was 100. On a straight dry road."

"Oh, we didn't go anywhere," Rodney said. "We used it for meetings." He stopped suddenly. "What's in the box?"

Harry handed the box to Derek because in that moment he could see where this was going, the woodworking co-op in Newtown, in that street – what did they call it now?– behind the Market Theatre. And the clandestine meetings at night in the VW bus, parked on the next street in the theatre parking lot, discussing the finer points of Marxism, making plans destined to die unfulfilled. All talk, no action.

He stood stupidly, trying not to remember, while Derek opened the box and carefully unwrapped the bottle. The operation drew the half-dozen guys away from their saws and sanders.

"I never knew you could do that," Rodney said.

"Nor did I," said Harry. Concentrate on the ship. Forget the co-op. These men would never understand. "I had a neighbour in Berea when I was a kid who showed me how to do this. A funny guy – I think he was Russian. Last year I had time on my hands, and so I gave it a whirl."

"How does that work?" asked a man who had been sawing planks. "Looks damned delicate."

"Not too bad when you know how. You just shouldn't rush it."

"Not like the old days, was it Harry? We were always in a rush. We had to be."

"Why would that be?" Derek asked.

"Orders," Harry said quickly. "We had a lot of orders."

"It would be interesting to watch you work," said the man of the planks. "Think you could make another one here?"

"I'd have to get the right wood and the material for the sails ... I wasn't sure I would ever make another one."

"You'd be doing us a great favour," Derek said. "How many toys can we make? How many table legs can we turn out before we have to move on, find another challenge?"

They seemed nice guys, genuinely interested, and in any case, the equipment on offer was attractive. There was even a row of chisels. "I'll see what I can find. So Rodney, what are you sanding over there?"

Harry finally got away, but not before agreeing to drop in on Rodney for a drink that afternoon. Or maybe the next day. Or not at all.

Back in his walled garden, a glass of pre-lunch merlot by his side and the Italian novel on his lap, he felt relaxed enough to revisit the life he'd carved out for himself since he'd left the workshop in the early 80s.

He'd gone to London to study art, but one year on, his mother was dying, he came home for the funeral, met Claire, stayed and picked up the old friendships that had gone dormant during his workshop days.

It was a pretty decent life – a wife, kids, friends, work he enjoyed and was good at. His mother had wanted him to go in for actuarial science, but he'd stuck with accountancy instead. It was easy to set up an office when he returned from London, and it suited him. It meant he could put deals together, which was satisfying, and it left his mind free for other pursuits, for example, discovering his ability to read the book currently open at page 25.

But concentration wasn't easy, not with hadedas sounding their unearthly calls on the other side of the wall, and Rodney digging up memories.

Rodney had remained at the Newtown workshop after he'd left, if his memory served, and so had a few of the banned unionists, and the guy who started it, plus a couple of others. A year or two later, he'd heard the place was deserted. Things were hotting up. The Struggle had begun in earnest.

These guys at the workshop next to the coffee shop wouldn't understand what it was like in those days. Sure, they were around, they couldn't have missed reading about the car bombs and noticing the heightened security, but they weren't hiding activists on the run. Nor were they teaching them how to attach a leg to a table, sand it smooth, stain it, sell it.

He picked the book up again and got to page 27 before the doorbell rang. He ignored it. Whoever it was – he suspected Rodney – rang twice more, than gave up.

It was the next morning that memories began to scratch at his consciousness, then slip away. He let them go. Who wants to remember those days?

He had just poured the coffee when the bell rang again. He cursed Rodney but judging from his performance the day before, he'd ring all morning, so he opened the door to stop him, and was surprised to see Derek standing there, although he shouldn't have been. It was turning into a habit.

"Still got that tea?" Derek said. "I'd love a cup."

This time he followed Harry into the kitchen. "This workshop of yours," he said. "That fellow you worked with. What's his name?"

"Rodney," Harry said, getting down the teapot.

"Said you chaps worked the mortice and tenon way. No screws, no glue. You know, there are easier ways to put furniture together."

"It took us a few weeks to get it right. We only made beds in the beginning," Harry said, remembering. "And coffins."

"Coffins?" Derek laughed. "This is the place for that. Get a good business going."

"And xylophones," Harry said quickly. "When we got better at it, we made desks. And tables, from railway sleepers." His coffee was getting cold. He shoved it into the microwave. "None of us knew anything. The guy who started it was a friend of mine, he taught us." Amazing guy. A carpenter with a master's in economics. "He taught a lot of people. Rodney. Me. His gardener – he brought him in."

It was all coming back now, hot and heavy, the smell of the place, an old warehouse formerly used to store mielie meal, the dust, the noise, the coughing …

"No extractor. No health and safety. We weren't registered. My chest seized up for years."

"You're all right now?"

"I left and went to England."

"That fellow who worked with you, he told me there wasn't much in the way of equipment."

"Oh, we had some stuff."

They walked into the living room, Derek with his tea, black, no milk, no sugar, and Harry with his rewarmed coffee.

"We bought some tools at auction – a couple of planers, a table saw, that kind of thing. It was a co-op."

"Sounds like what we have down by the coffee shop," Derek said, took a sip, then put the tea down on the coffee table and settled in on the couch. "Of course we don't have meetings in a Volkswagen bus in the dead of night. What were you chaps up to anyway? Planning to overthrow the government?"

There, it was out. "Not really," Harry said carefully. "Just ... we'd all been in the army. What we'd seen – it was disgusting. Worse. Horrible."

"Your friend told me you had banned men among you."

Harry didn't know what to say. So he just drank his coffee.

"Back in the day," Derek said, "my good wife was a member of the Black Sash. I lived in terror that she would bring home some saboteur on the run."

He took a sip of tea as Harry watched him, struck dumb.

"Funnily enough, it was her brother who snuck in a young Zulu fellow who needed somewhere to hide. A nice chap once you got to know him. We stashed him in my son's room for a week. He was waiting for safe passage ... I think it was Botswana? Maybe Zimbabwe. Tanzania. I don't know. It was a long time ago.

"He'd had a terrible life, this chap. He'd grown up in poverty I couldn't imagine. The stories ... He'd seen his brother kicked to death by police, had to leave school at fifteen.

"I can tell you, Harry, by the time he was collected by the chaps he called his comrades, I was almost ready to take up arms myself. I wonder where young Thabo is now. Probably in parliament. Or taking home sacks of money out of one of those, what are they called? State-owned enterprises."

He laughed. And so did Harry.

Later, sitting in the garden trying to get past page 27, Harry wondered why he'd agreed when Derek suggested they go together to find wood for a simple sailboat in a bottle. "Or an aircraft carrier," Derek had suggested, before drinking the rest of the tea and rising to take the cup back to the kitchen.

"I suppose we look like nothing more than a collection of old fogeys," he'd said, standing at the front door. "Fogeys – that's the polite term. Old farts is what they call us. But you'd be surprised at what some of the chaps got up to in their youth."

Harry agreed to show the guys in the workshop how to build a ship in a bottle. Word got out and on the day a large crowd watched him insert the boat, then raise the sails. More men joined the workshop during the next few days, claiming they hadn't known the place existed. The coffee machine had quite a workout.

Harry, to his horror, became a minor celebrity, recognised by other residents. It was not pleasant. When encountered on the path to his cottage and, naturally, greeted, his response was a hand raised in acknowledgement and sometimes a brief nod, sometimes a grunt.

Not surprisingly, Harry never hosted drinks for his neighbours, or attended open house events, or meet-and-greet braais on Sunday afternoons. His main social event continued to be the fortnightly poker school.

However, once in a while he went across the way to Derek and Julie for supper. She was a terrific cook, and the food was better than Woolworth's frozen meals.

If only she'd leave off the matchmaking. Although there was one friend of hers, came to supper a few times. A retired schoolteacher, a good conversationalist, knew a lot about art. What was her name? Something biblical ... Ruth? No. ... Miriam? Not sure ... Maybe Esther?

Maybe.

Acknowledgements

It takes if not a village at least a neighbourhood to produce a book – advice and encouragement from friends, information from experts, help from early readers. *Moving On* needed all of that, and more.

Thanks to Pat Tucker, editor extraordinaire, without whom there would have been no book.

I'm grateful for advice, much of which I followed, and for information in the course of research from, in no particular order, Tanya Pampalone, Marilyn Honikman, Maud Motanyane, Jenni Lazarow, Rosa Manoim, Thando Maurice, Patience Seydou, Clive Cope, Julia Grey, and Mac Carrim, whose manuscript on living with a partner with Alzheimer's should be required reading for anyone in that difficult situation.

Thank you to the people who shared their experiences.

And many thanks to Modjaji Books founder and publisher Colleen Higgs, whose excellent list I am proud to join.